Heinrich von Kleist
Michael Kohlhaas

GERMAN CLASSICS

Heinrich von Kleist

Michael Kohlhaas
A Tale from an Old Chronicle

Translated by
Frances H. King

With an essay about
"The Life of Heinrich von Kleist" by
John S. Nollen

MONDIAL

Mondial
New York

Heinrich von Kleist:
Michael Kohlhaas. A Tale from an Old Chronicle
(1808)

With an essay about "The Life of Heinrich von Kleist"
(ca. 1914) by John S. Nollen

Translated by Frances H. King

ISBN 978-1-59569-076-0

Library of Congress Control Number: 2007940790

www.mondialbooks.com

the army and entered upon his brief course as a student in his native city. He applied himself with laborious zeal to the mastery of a wide range of subjects, and hastened, with pedantic gravity, to retail his newly won learning to his sisters and a group of their friends. For the time being, the impulse of self-expression took this didactic turn, which is very prominent also in his correspondence. Within the year he was betrothed to a member of this informal class, Wilhelmina von Zenge, the daughter of an officer. The question of a career now crowded out his interest in study; in August, 1800, as a step toward the solution of this problem, Kleist returned to Berlin and secured a modest appointment in the customs department. He found no more satisfaction in the civil than in his former military service, and all manner of vague plans, artistic, literary and academic, occupied his mind. Intensive study of Kant's philosophy brought on an intellectual crisis, in which the ardent student found himself bereft of his fond hope of attaining to absolute truth. Meanwhile the romantic appeal of Nature, first heeded on a trip to Würzburg, and the romantic lure of travel, drew the dreamer irresistibly away from his desk. His sister Ulrica accompanied him on a journey that began in April, 1801, and brought them, by a devious route, to Paris in July. By this time Kleist had become clearly conscious of his vocation; the strong creative impulse that had hitherto bewildered him now found its proper vent in poetic expression, and he felt himself dedicated to a literary career. With characteristic secretiveness he kept hidden, even from his sister, the drama at which he was quietly working.

Absorbed in his new ambition, Kleist found little in Paris to interest him. He felt the need of solitude for the maturing of his plans, and with the double object of seeking in idyllic pursuits the inspiration of Nature and of earning leisure for writing, he proposed to his betrothed that she join him secretly in establishing a home upon a small farm in Switzerland. When Wilhelmina found it impossible to accept this plan, Kleist coldly severed all relations with her. He journeyed to Switzerland in December, 1801, and in Bern became acquainted with a group of young authors, the novelist Heinrich Zschokke, the publisher Heinrich Gessner, and Ludwig Wieland, son of the famous author of *Oberon*. To these sympathetic friends he read his first tragedy, which, in its earlier draft, had a Spanish setting, as *The Thierrez Family* or *The Ghonorez Family*, but which, on their advice, was given a German background. This drama Gessner published for Kleist, under the title *The Schroffenstein Family*, in the winter of 1802-03. It had no sooner appeared than the author felt himself to have outgrown its youthful weaknesses of imitation and exaggeration. Another dramatic production grew directly out of the discussions of this little circle. The friends agreed, on a wager, to put into literary form the story suggested by an engraving that hung in Zschokke's room. By common consent the prize was awarded to Kleist's production, his one comedy, *The Broken Jug*.

In April, 1802, Kleist realized his romantic dream by taking up his abode, in rural seclusion, on a little island at the outlet of the Lake of Thun, amid the majestic scenery of the Bernese Oberland. In this retreat, encouraged by the applause of his first confidants, he labored with joyous energy, recasting his *Schroffenstein Family*, working out the *Broken Jug*, meditating historical dramas on Leopold of Austria and Peter the Hermit, and expending the best of his untrained genius on the plan of a tragedy, *Robert Guiscard*, in which he strove to create a drama of a new type, combining the beauties of Greek classical art and of Shakespeare; with his *Guiscard* the young poet even dared hope to "snatch the laurel wreath from Goethe's brow."

Two months of intense mental exertion in the seclusion of his island left Kleist exhausted, and he fell seriously ill; whereupon Ulrica, on receiving belated news of his plight, hastened to Bern to care for him. When a political revolution drove Ludwig Wieland from Bern, they followed the latter to Weimar, where the poet Wieland, the dean of the remarkable group of great authors gathered at Weimar, received Kleist kindly, and made him his guest at his country estate. With great difficulty Wieland succeeded in persuading his secretive visitor to reveal his literary plans; and when Kleist recited from memory some of the scenes of his unfinished *Guiscard*, the old poet was transported with enthusiasm; these fragments seemed to him worthy of the united genius of Æschylus, Sophocles, and Shakespeare, and he was convinced that Kleist had the power to "fill the void in the history of the German drama that even Goethe and Schiller had not filled." But in spite of Wieland's generous encouragement, Kleist found it impossible to complete this masterpiece, and his hopeless pursuit of the perfect ideal became an intolerable obsession to his ambitious and sensitive soul. He could not remain in Weimar. In Dresden old friends sought to cheer him in his desperate attempts to seize the elusive ideal; to more than one of them, in his despair, he proposed a joint suicide. Again he was driven to seek solace and inspiration in travel, a friend accompanying him to

III

Switzerland. Arrived at Geneva in October, 1803, Kleist fell into the deepest despondency, and wrote Ulrica a letter full of hopeless renunciation. Half crazed by disappointment and wounded pride, he rushed madly through France to Paris, broke with his friend, who had again repelled a joint suicide, burned his manuscript of *Guiscard*, and made secretly for Boulogne, hoping to find an honorable death in Napoleon's projected invasion of England. Fortunately he fell in with an acquaintance who saved him from the risk of being arrested as a spy, and started him back on his homeward way. He was detained at Mentz by serious illness, but finally, in June, 1804, reappeared in Potsdam. The poet's spirit was broken, and he was glad to accept a petty civil post that took him to Königsberg. After a year of quiet work, he was enabled, by a small pension from Queen Louise, to resign his office and again devote himself to literature.

The two years spent in Königsberg were years of remarkable development in Kleist's literary power. Warned by the catastrophe of the earlier attempt to reach the heights at a single bound, he now schooled himself with simpler tasks: adaptations, from the French, of La Fontaine's poem, *The two Pigeons*, and of Molière's comedy, *Amphitryon* both so altered in the interpretation that they seem more like originals than translations; prose tales that are admirable examples of this form, *The Marquise of O.*, *The Earthquake in Chili*, and the first part of the masterly short story *Michael Kohlhaas*; and the recasting of the unique comedy *The Broken Jug*. Finally he attempted another great drama in verse, *Penthesilea*, embodying in the old classical story the tragedy of his own desperate struggle for *Guiscard*, and his crushing defeat.

Meanwhile the clouds were gathering about his beloved country, and in October, 1806, the thunderbolt fell in the rout of the Prussian army at Jena. Napoleon's victorious troops pressed on to Berlin, and the Prussian court retreated with the tide of fugitives to Königsberg. Kleist was overwhelmed by the misery of this cataclysm, which, however, he had clearly foreseen and foretold. With a group of friends he started on foot for Dresden, but was arrested as a spy at the gates of Berlin and held for months as a prisoner in French fortresses, before the energetic efforts of Ulrica and others procured his release.

Late in July, 1807, he finally arrived in Dresden, where he remained until April, 1809. These were the happiest and the most prolific months of his fragmentary life. The best literary and social circles of the Saxon capital were open to him, his talent was recognized

IV

by the leading men of the city, a laurel wreath was placed upon his brow by "the prettiest hands in Dresden;" at last he found all his hopes being realized. With three friends he embarked on an ambitious publishing enterprise, which included the issuing of a sumptuous literary and artistic monthly, the *Phœbus*. This venture was foredoomed to failure by the inexperience of its projectors and by the unsettled condition of a time full of political upheaval and most unfavorable to any literary enterprise. Kleist's own contributions to this periodical were of the highest value; here appeared first in print generous portions of *Penthesilea, The Broken Jug*, and the new drama *Kitty of Heilbronn*, the first act of the ill-fated *Robert Guiscard*, evidently reproduced from memory, *The Marquise of O.*, and part of *Michael Kohlhaas*. If we add to these works the great patriotic drama, *Arminius (Die Hermannsschlacht)*, two tales, *The Betrothal in San Domingo* and *The Foundling*, and lyric and narrative poems, the production of the brief period in Dresden is seen to bulk very large.

In the stress of the times and in spite of the most strenuous efforts, the *Phœbus* went under with the first volume, and the publishing business was a total wreck. Kleist's joy at the acceptance of *The Broken Jug* by Goethe for the Weimar theatre was turned to bitterness when, because of unintelligent acting and stage management, this brilliant comedy failed wretchedly; the disappointed author held Goethe responsible for this fiasco and foolishly attacked him in a series of spiteful epigrams. He longed to have his *Arminius* performed at Vienna, but the Austrian authorities were too timid to risk the production of a play that openly preached German unity and a war of revenge against the "Roman tyranny" of Napoleon. Kleist then turned to lyric poetry and polemic tirades for the expression of his patriotic ardor. When Austria rose against Napoleon, he started for the seat of war and was soon the happy eye-witness of the Austrian victory at Aspern, in May, 1809. In Prague, with the support of the commandant, he planned a patriotic journal, for which he immediately wrote a series of glowing articles, mostly in the form of political satires. This plan was wrecked by the decisive defeat of the Austrians at Wagram in July.

Broken by these successive disasters, Kleist again fell seriously ill; for four months his friends had no word from him, and reports of his death were current. In November, 1809, he came to Frankfort-on-the-Oder to dispose of his share in the family home as a last means of raising funds, and again disappeared. In January, 1810, he

V

passed through Frankfort on the way to Berlin, to which the Prussian court, now subservient to Napoleon, had returned. He found many old friends in Berlin, and even had prospects of recognition from the court, as the brave and beautiful Queen Louise was very kindly disposed toward him. Again he turned to dramatic production, and in the patriotic Prussian play, *Prince Frederick of Homburg*, created his masterpiece. Fortune seemed once more to be smiling upon the dramatist; the *Prince of Homburg* was to be dedicated to Queen Louise, and performed privately at the palace of Prince Radziwill, before being given at the National Theatre. But again the cup of success was dashed from the poet's lips. With the death of Queen Louise, in July, 1810, he lost his only powerful friend at court, and now found it impossible to get a hearing for his drama.

Other disappointments came in rapid succession. *Kitty of Heilbronn*, performed after many delays at Vienna, was not a success, and Iffland, the popular dramatist and director of the Berlin Theatre, rejected this play, while accepting all manner of commonplace works by inferior authors. The famous publisher Cotta did print Penthesilea, but was so displeased with it that he made no effort to sell the edition, and *Kitty of Heilbronn*, declined by Cotta, fell flat when it was printed in Berlin. Two volumes of tales, including some masterpieces in this form, hardly fared better; the new numbers in this collection were *The Duel*, *The Beggar Woman of Locarno*, and *Saint Cecilia*. Again the much-tried poet turned to journalism. From October, 1810, until March, 1811, with the assistance of the popular philosopher Adam Müller and the well-known romantic authors Arnim, Brentano, and Fouqué, he published a politico-literary journal appearing five times a week. The enterprise began well, and aroused a great deal of interest. Gradually, however, the censorship of a government that was at once timid and tyrannical limited the scope and destroyed the effectiveness of the paper, and Kleist spent himself in vain efforts to keep it alive. The poet now found himself in a desperate predicament, financially ruined by the failure of all his enterprises, and discredited with the government, from which he vainly sought some reparation for the violence done to his journal; worst of all, he found himself without honor at home, where he was looked upon as a ne'er-do-well and a disgrace to the reputation of a fine old military family. As a last resort he applied for reinstatement in the army, it being a time when Prussia seemed to be girding herself for another struggle with Napoleon. But the attempt to borrow enough money for his military equip-

VI

ment failed, and he found no sympathy or support on a final visit to his family in Frankfort. In October, 1811, the patriotic men who had been quietly preparing for the inevitable war of liberation were horrified by the movement of the Prussian government toward another alliance with Napoleon; and Kleist felt it impossible to enter an army that might at any moment be ordered to support the arch-enemy of his country. His case had become utterly hopeless.

At this juncture the unfortunate poet found what he had so often sought in his crises of despair—a companion in suicide. Through Adam Müller he had become acquainted with Henrietta Vogel, an intelligent woman of romantic temperament, who was doomed by an incurable disease to a life of suffering. She listened eagerly to Kleist's suggestions of an escape together from the intolerable ills of life. The two drove from Berlin to a solitary inn on the shore of the Wannsee, near Potsdam; here Kleist wrote a touching farewell letter to his sister, and, on the afternoon of November 21, 1811, after the most deliberate preparations, the companions strolled into the silent pine woods, where Kleist took Henrietta's life and then his own. In the same lonely place his grave was dug, and here the greatest Prussian poet lay forgotten, after the brief, though violent, sensation of his tragic end; half a century elapsed before a Prussian prince set up a simple granite monument to mark the grave. Ten years passed after Kleist's death before his last great dramas, *Arminius* and the *Prince of Homburg*, were published, edited by the eminent poet and critic Ludwig Tieck, who also brought out, in 1826, the first collection of Kleist's works. Long before this time, the patriotic uprising for which he had labored with desperate zeal in his later works, had brought liberation to Germany; it was on the thirty-sixth anniversary of Kleist's birth that Napoleon's power was shaken by the decisive Battle of Leipzig.

Heinrich von Kleist was born into a generation that was dominated by the spirit of Romanticism. Tieck and the Schlegels were a few years older, Fouqué was of the same age as he, and Arnim and Brentano somewhat younger. His acquaintance was largely with the authors who represented this tendency. In his own works, however, Kleist was singularly independent of the romantic influence. This is the more remarkable inasmuch as his character had many traits in common with the ardent spirits of the Romantic group. His uncompromising individualism and overweening ambition, his love of travel, his enthusiastic acceptance of Rousseau's gospel of Nature, are characteristically Romantic, and so, we may say, is his passionate patriotism. Eccentricities he had in plenty; there was something morbid in his excessive reserve, his exaggerated secretiveness about the most important interests of his life, as there surely was in his moroseness, which deepened at times into black despair. Goethe was most unpleasantly impressed by this abnormal quality of Kleist's personality, and said of the younger poet: "In spite of my honest desire to sympathize with him, I could not avoid a feeling of horror and loathing, as of a body beautifully endowed by nature, but infected with an incurable disease." That this judgment was unduly harsh is evident enough from the confidence and affection that Kleist inspired in many of the best men of his time.

Whatever may have been Kleist's personal peculiarities, his works give evidence of the finest artistic sanity and conscience. His acute sense of literary form sets him off from the whole generation of Romanticists, who held the author's personal caprice to be the supreme law of poetry, and most of whose important works were either medleys or fragments. He was his own severest critic, and labored over his productions, as he did over his own education, with untiring energy and intense concentration. A less scrupulous author would not have destroyed the manuscript of *Robert Guiscard* because he could not keep throughout its action the splendid promise of the first act. His works are usually marked by rare logical and artistic consistency. Seldom is there any interruption of the unity and simple directness of his actions by sub-plots or episodes, and he scorned the easy theatrical devices by which the successful playwrights of his day gained their effects. Whether in drama or story, his action grows naturally out of the characters and the situations. Hence the marvelous fact that his dramas can be performed with hardly an alteration, though the author, never having seen any of them on the stage, lacked the practical experience by which most dramatists learn the technique of their art.

Kleist evidently studied the models of classical art with care. His unerring sense of form, his artistic restraint in a day when caprice was the ruling fashion, and the conciseness of his expression, are doubtless due to classical influence. But, at the same time, he was an innovator, one of the first forerunners of modern realism. He describes and characterizes with careful, often microscopic detail; his psychological analysis is remarkably exact and incisive; and he fearlessly uses the ugly or the trivial when either better serves his purpose.

In all the varied volume of Kleist's works, there is very little that is mediocre or negligible. *The Schroffenstein Family*, to be sure, is prentice work, but it can bear comparison with the first plays of the greatest dramatists. The fragment of *Robert Guiscard* is masterly in its rapid cumulative exposition, representing the hero, idolized by his troops, as stricken with the plague when the crowning glory of his military career seems to be within his grasp; while the discord between Guiscard's son and nephew presages an irrepressible family conflict. The style, as Wieland felt when he listened with rapture to the author's recital, is a blend of classical and Elizabethan art. The opening chorus of the people, the formal balanced speeches, the analytical action, beginning on the verge of the catastrophe, are traits borrowed from Greek tragedy. On the other hand, there is much realistic characterization and a Shakespearian variety and freedom of tone. *The Broken Jug*, too, is analytical in its conduct. Almost from the first it is evident that Adam, the village judge, is himself the culprit in the case at trial in his court, and the comic efforts of the archrascal to squirm out of the inevitable discovery only serve to make his guilt the surer. In this comedy the blank verse adapts itself to all the turns of familiar humorous dialogue, and the effect of the Dutch genre-paintings of Teniers or Jan Steen is admirably reproduced in dramatic form. The slowly moving action, constantly reverting to past incidents, makes a successful performance difficult; the fate of this work on the stage has depended upon finding an actor capable of bringing out all the possibilities in the part of Adam, who is a masterpiece of comic self-characterization.

Penthesilea is a work apart. Passionate, headlong, almost savage, is the character of the queen of the Amazons, yet wonderfully sweet in its gentler moods and glorified with the golden glow of high poetry. Nothing could be further removed from the pseudo-classical manner of the eighteenth century than this modern and individual interpretation of the old mythical story of Penthesilea and Achilles, between whom love breaks forth in the midst of mortal combat. The clash of passions creates scenes in this drama that transcend the humanly and dramatically permissible. Yet there is a wealth of imaginative beauty and emotional melody in this tragedy beyond anything in Kleist's other works. It was written with his heart's blood; in it he uttered all the yearning and frenzy of his first passion for the unattainable and ruined masterpiece Guiscard.

Kitty of Heilbronn stands almost at the opposite pole from *Penthesilea*. The pathos of Griselda's unquestioning self-abnegation is her portion; she is the extreme expression of the docile quality that

Kleist sought in his betrothed. Instead of the fabled scenes of Homeric combat, we have here as a setting the richly romantic and colorful life of the age of chivalry. The form, too, is far freer and more expansive, with an unconventional mingling of verse and prose.

The last two plays were born of the spirit that brought forth the War of Liberation. In them Kleist gave undying expression to his ardent patriotism; it was his deepest grief that these martial dramas were not permitted to sound their trumpet-call to a humbled nation yearning to be free. *Arminius* is a great dramatized philippic. The ancient Germanic chiefs Marbod and Arminius, representing in Kleist's intention the Austria and Prussia of his day, are animated by one common patriotic impulse, rising far above their mutual rivalries, to cast off the hateful and oppressive yoke of Rome; and after the decisive victory over Varus in the Teutoburg Forest, each of these strong chiefs is ready in devoted self-denial to yield the primacy to the other, in order that all Germans may stand together against the common foe. *Prince Frederick of Homburg* is a dramatic glorification of the Prussian virtues of discipline and obedience. But the finely drawn characters of this play are by no means rigid martinets. They are largely, frankly, generously human, confessing the right of feeling as well as reason to direct the will. Never has there been a more sympathetic literary exposition of the soldierly character than this last tribute of a devoted patriot to his beloved Brandenburg.

The narrative works of Kleist maintain the same high level as his dramas. *Michael Kohlhaas* is a good example of this excellent narrative art, for which Kleist found no models in German literature. Unity is a striking characteristic; the action can usually be summed up in a few words, such as the formula for this story, given expressly on its first page: "His sense of justice made him a robber and a murderer." There is no leisurely exposition of time, place, or situation; all the necessary elements are given concisely in the first sentences. The action develops logically, with effective use of retardation and climax, but without disturbing episodes; and the reader is never permitted to forget the central theme. The descriptive element is realistic, with only pertinent details swiftly presented, often in parentheses, while the action moves on. The characterization is skilfully indirect, through unconscious action and speech. The author does not shun the trivial or even the repulsive in detail, nor does he fear the most tragic catastrophes. He is scrupulously objective, and, in an age of expansive lyric expression, he is most chary of comment. The sentence structure, as in the dramas, is often intricate, but never lax. The whole work in all its parts is firmly and finely forged by a master workman.

Kleist has remained a solitary figure in German literature. Owing little to the dominant literary influences of his day, he has also found few imitators. Two generations passed before he began to come into his heritage of legitimate fame. Now that a full century has elapsed since his tragic death, his place is well assured among the greatest dramatic and narrative authors of Germany. A brave man struggling desperately against hopeless odds, a patriot expending his genius with lavish unselfishness for the service of his country in her darkest days, he has been found worthy by posterity to stand as the most famous son of a faithful Prussian family of soldiers.

(ca. 1914)

MICHAEL KOHLHAAS
A Tale from an Old Chronicle

Toward the middle of the sixteenth century there lived on the banks of the river Havel a horse-dealer by the name of Michael Kohlhaas, the son of a school-master, one of the most upright and, at the same time, one of the most terrible men of his day. Up to his thirtieth year this extraordinary man would have been considered the model of a good citizen. In a village which still bears his name, he owned a farmstead on which he quietly supported himself by plying his trade. The children with whom his wife presented him were brought up in the fear of God, and taught to be industrious and honest; nor was there one among his neighbors who had not enjoyed the benefit of his kindness or his justice. In short, the world would have had every reason to bless his memory if he had not carried to excess one virtue— his sense of justice, which made of him a robber and a murderer.

He rode abroad once with a string of young horses, all well fed and glossy-coated, and was turning over in his mind how he would employ the profit that he hoped to make from them at the fairs; part of it, as is the way with good managers, he would use to gain future profits, but he would also spend part of it in the enjoyment of the present. While thus engaged he reached the Elbe, and near a stately castle, situated on Saxon territory, he came upon a toll-bar which he had never found on this road before. Just in the midst of a heavy shower he halted with his horses and called to the toll-gate keeper, who soon after showed his surly face at the window. The horse-dealer told him to open the gate. "What new arrangement is this?" he asked, when the toll-gatherer, after some time, finally came out of the house.

"Seignorial privilege," answered the latter, unlocking the gate, "conferred by the sovereign upon Squire Wenzel Tronka."

"Is that so?" queried Kohlhaas; "the Squire's name is now Wenzel?" and gazed at the castle, the glittering battlements of which looked out over the field. "Is the old gentleman dead?"

"Died of apoplexy," answered the gate keeper, as he raised the toll-bar.

"Hum! Too bad!" rejoined Kohlhaas. "An estimable old gentleman he was, who liked to watch people come and go, and helped along trade and traffic wherever he could. He once had a causeway built because a mare of mine had broken her leg out there on the road leading to the village. Well, how much is it?" he asked, and with some trouble got out the few groschen demanded by the gate keeper from under his cloak, which was fluttering in the wind. "Yes, old man," he added, picking up the leading reins as the latter muttered "Quick, quick!" and cursed the weather; "if this tree had remained standing in the forest it would have been better for me and for you." With this he gave him the money, and started to ride on.

He had hardly passed under the toll-bar, however, when a new voice cried out from the tower behind him, "Stop there, horse-dealer!" and he saw the castellan close a window and come hurrying down to him. "Well, I wonder what he wants!" Kohlhaas asked himself, and halted with his horses. Buttoning another waistcoat over his ample body, the castellan came up to him and, standing with his back to the storm, demanded his passport.

"My passport?" queried Kohlhaas. Somewhat disconcerted, he replied that he had none, so far as he knew, but that, if some one would just describe to him what in the name of goodness this was, perhaps he might accidentally happen to have one about him. The castellan, eying him askance, retorted that without an official permit no horse-dealer was allowed to cross the border with horses. The horse-dealer assured him that seventeen times in his life he had crossed the border without such a permit; that he was well acquainted with all the official regulations which applied to his trade; that this would probably prove to be only a mistake; the castellan would please consider the matter and, since he had a long day's journey before him, not detain him here unnecessarily any longer. But the castellan answered that he was not going to slip through the eighteenth time, that the ordinance concerning this matter had been only recently issued, and that he must either procure the passport here or go back to the place from which he had come. After a moment's reflection, the horse-dealer, who was beginning to feel bitter, got down from his horse, turned it over to a groom, and said that he would speak to Squire Tronka himself on the subject. He really did walk toward the castle; the castellan followed him, muttering something about niggardly money-grubbers, and what a good thing it was to bleed them; and, measuring each other with their glances, the two entered the castle-hall.

It happened that the Squire was sitting over his wine with some merry friends, and a joke had caused them all to break into uproarious laughter just as Kohlhaas approached him to make his complaint. The Squire asked what he wanted; the young nobles, at sight of the stranger, became silent; but no sooner had the latter broached his request concerning the horses, than the whole group cried out, "Horses! Where are they?" and hurried over to the window to look at them. When they saw the glossy string, they all followed the suggestion of the Squire and flew down into the courtyard. The rain had ceased; the castellan, the steward, and the servant gathered round them and all scanned the horses. One praised a bright bay with a white star on its forehead, another preferred a chestnut, a third patted the dappled horse with tawny spots; and all were of the opinion that the horses were like deer, and that no finer were raised in the country. Kohlhaas answered cheerily that the horses were no better than the knights who were to ride them, and invited the men to buy. The Squire, who eagerly desired the big bay stallion, went so far as to ask its price, and the steward urged him to buy a pair of black horses, which he thought he could use on the farm, as they were short of horses. But when the horse-dealer had named his price the young knights thought it too high, and the Squire said that Kohlhaas would have to ride in search of the Round Table and King Arthur if he put such a high value on his horses. Kohlhaas noticed that the castellan and the steward were whispering together and casting significant glances at the black horses the while, and, moved by a vague presentiment, made every effort to sell them the horses. He said to the Squire, "Sir, I bought those black horses six months ago for twenty-five gold gulden; give me thirty and you shall have them." Two of the young noblemen who were standing beside the Squire declared quite audibly that the horses were probably worth that much; but the Squire said that while he might be willing to pay out money for the bay stallion, he really should hardly care to do so for the pair of blacks, and prepared to go in. Whereupon Kohlhaas, saying that the next time he came that way with his horses they might perhaps strike a bargain, took leave of the Squire and, seizing the reins of his horse, started to ride away.

At this moment the castellan stepped forth from the crowd and reminded him that he would not be allowed to leave without a passport. Kohlhaas turned around and inquired of the Squire whether this statement, which meant the ruin of his whole trade, were indeed correct. The Squire, as he went off, answered with an embarrassed air, "Yes, Kohlhaas, you must get a passport. Speak to the castellan about it, and go your way." Kohlhaas assured him that he had not the least intention of evading the ordinances which might be in force concerning the exportation of horses. He promised that when he went through Dresden he would take out the passport at the chancery, and begged to be allowed to go on, this time, as he had known nothing whatever about this requirement. "Well!" said the Squire, as the storm at that moment began to rage again and the wind blustered about his scrawny legs; "let the wretch go. Come!" he added to the young knights, and, turning around, started toward the door. The castellan, facing about toward the Squire, said that Kohlhaas must at least leave behind some pledge as security that he would obtain the passport. The Squire stopped again under the castle gate. Kohlhaas asked how much security for the black horses in money or in articles of value he would be expected to leave. The steward muttered in his beard that he might just as well leave the blacks themselves.

"To be sure," said the castellan; "that is the best plan; as soon as he has taken out the passport he can come and get them again at any time." Kohlhaas, amazed at such a shameless demand, told the Squire, who was holding the skirts of his doublet about him for warmth, that what he wanted to do was to sell the blacks; but as a gust of wind just then blew a torrent of rain and hail through the gate, the Squire, in order to put an end to the matter, called out, "If he won't give up the horses, throw him back again over the toll-bar;" and with that he went off.

The horse-dealer, who saw clearly that on this occasion he would have to yield to superior force, made up his mind to comply with the demand, since there really was no other way out of it. He unhitched the black horses and led them into a stable which the castellan pointed out to him. He left a groom in charge of them, provided him with money, warned him to take good care of the horses until he came back, and with the rest of the string continued his journey to Leipzig, where he purposed to go to the fair. As he rode along he wondered, in half uncertainty, whether after all such a law might not have been passed in Saxony for the protection of the newly started industry of horse-raising.

On his arrival in Dresden, where, in one of the suburbs of the city, he owned a house and stable—this being the headquarters from which he usually conducted his business at the smaller fairs around the country—he went immediately to the chancery. And here he learned from the councilors, some of whom he knew, that indeed, as his first instinct had already told him, the story of the passport was only made up. At Kohlhaas's request, the annoyed councilors gave him a written certificate of its baselessness, and the horse-dealer smiled at the lean Squire's joke, although he did not quite see what purpose he could have had in view. A few weeks later, having sold to his satisfaction the string of horses he had with him, Kohlhaas returned to Tronka Castle harboring no other resentment save that caused by the general misery of the world.

The castellan, to whom he showed the certificate, made no comment upon it, and to the horse-dealer's question as to whether he could now have his horses back, replied that he need only go down to the stable and get them. But even while crossing the courtyard, Kohlhaas learned with dismay that for alleged insolence his groom had been cudgeled and dismissed in disgrace a few days after being left behind at Tronka Castle. Of the boy who informed him of this he inquired what in the world the groom had done, and who had taken care of the horses in the mean time; to this the boy answered that he did not know, and then opened to the horse-dealer, whose heart was already full of misgivings, the door of the stable in which the horses stood. How great, though, was his astonishment when, instead of his two glossy, well-fed blacks, he spied a pair of lean, worn-out jades, with bones on which one could have hung things as if on pegs, and with mane and hair matted together from lack of care and attention—in short, the very picture of utter misery in the animal kingdom! Kohlhaas, at the sight of whom the horses neighed and moved feebly, was extremely indignant, and asked what had happened to his horses. The boy, who was standing beside him, answered that they had not suffered any harm, and that they had had proper feed too, but, as it had been harvest time, they had been used a bit in the fields because there weren't draught animals enough. Kohlhaas cursed over the shameful, preconcerted outrage; but realizing that he was powerless he suppressed his rage, and, as no other course lay open to him, was preparing to leave this den of thieves again with his horses when the castellan, attracted by the altercation, appeared and asked what was the matter.

"What's the matter?" echoed Kohlhaas. "Who gave Squire Tronka and his people permission to use for work in the fields the black horses that I left behind with him?" He added, "Do you call that humane?" and trying to rouse the exhausted nags with a switch, he showed him that they did not move. The castellan, after he had watched him for a while with an expression of defiance, broke out,

"Look at the ruffian! Ought not the churl to thank God that the jades are still alive!" He asked who would have been expected to take care of them when the groom had run away, and whether it were not just that the horses should have worked in the fields for their feed. He concluded by saying that Kohlhaas had better not make a rumpus or he would call the dogs and with them would manage to restore order in the courtyard.

The horse-dealer's heart thumped against his doublet. He felt a strong desire to throw the good-for-nothing, potbellied scoundrel into the mud and set his foot on his copper-colored face. But his sense of justice, which was as delicate as a gold-balance, still wavered; he was not yet quite sure before the bar of his own conscience whether his adversary were really guilty of a crime. And so, swallowing the abusive words and going over to the horses, he silently pondered the circumstances while arranging their manes, and asked in a subdued voice for what fault the groom had been turned out of the castle. The castellan replied, "Because the rascal was insolent in the courtyard; because he opposed a necessary change of stables and demanded that the horses of two young noblemen, who came to the castle, should, for the sake of his nags, be left out on the open highroad over night."

Kohlhaas would have given the value of the horses if he could have had the groom at hand to compare his statement with that of this thick-lipped castellan. He was still standing, straightening the tangled manes of the black horses, and wondering what could be done in the situation in which he found himself, when suddenly the scene changed, and Squire Wenzel Tronka, returning from hare-hunting, dashed into the courtyard, followed by a swarm of knights, grooms, and dogs. The castellan, when asked what had happened, immediately began to speak, and while, on the one hand, the dogs set up a murderous howl at the sight of the stranger, and, on the other, the knights sought to quiet them, he gave the Squire a maliciously garbled account of the turmoil the horse-dealer was making because his black horses had been used a little. He said, with a scornful laugh, that the horse-dealer refused to recognize the horses as his own.

Kohlhaas cried, "Your worship, those are not my horses. Those are not the horses which were worth thirty gold gulden! I want my well-fed, sound horses back again!"

The Squire, whose face grew momentarily pale, got down from his horse and said, "If the d—d scoundrel doesn't want to take the horses back, let him leave them here. Come, Gunther!" he called; "Hans, come!" He brushed the dust off his breeches with his hand and, just as he reached the door with the young knights, called "Bring wine!" and strode into the house.

Kohlhaas said that he would rather call the knacker and have his horses thrown into the carrion pit than lead them back, in that condition, to his stable at Kohlhaasenbrück. Without bothering himself further about the nags, he left them standing where they were, and, declaring that he should know how to get his rights, mounted his bay horse and rode away.

He was already galloping at full speed on the road to Dresden when, at the thought of the groom and of the complaint which had been made against him at the castle, he slowed down to a walk, and, before he had gone a thousand paces farther, turned his horse around again and took the road toward Kohlhaasenbrück, in order, as seemed to him wise and just, to hear first what the groom had to say. For in spite of the injuries he had suffered, a correct instinct, already familiar with the imperfect organization of the world, inclined him to put up with the loss of the horses and to regard it as a just consequence of the groom's misconduct in case there really could be imputed to the latter any such fault as the castellan charged. On the other hand, an equally admirable feeling took deeper and deeper root the farther he rode, hearing at every stop of the outrages perpetrated daily upon travelers at Tronka Castle; this instinct told him that if, as seemed probable, the whole incident proved to be a preconcerted plot, it was his duty to the world to make every effort to obtain for himself satisfaction for the injury suffered, and for his fellow-countrymen a guarantee against similar injuries in the future.

On his arrival at Kohlhaasenbrück, as soon as he had embraced his faithful wife Lisbeth and had kissed his children, who were shouting joyfully about his knees, he asked at once after Herse, the head groom, and whether anything had been heard from him. Lisbeth answered, "Oh yes, dearest Michael—that Herse! Just think! The poor fellow arrived here about a fortnight ago, most pitifully bruised and beaten; really, he was so battered that he couldn't even breathe freely. We put him to bed, where he kept coughing up blood, and after repeated questions we heard a story that no one could understand. He told us that you had left him at Tronka Castle in charge of some horses which they would not allow to pass through there, that by the most shameful maltreatment he had been forced to leave the castle, and that it had been impossible for him to bring the horses with him."

"Really!" exclaimed Kohlhaas, taking off his cloak. "I suppose he has recovered before this?"

"Pretty well, except that he still coughs blood," she answered. "I wanted to send another groom at once to Tronka Castle so as to have the horses taken care of until you got back there; for as Herse has always shown himself truthful and, indeed, more faithful to us than any other has ever been. I felt I had no right to doubt his statement, especially when confirmed by so many bruises, or to think that perhaps he had lost the horses in some other way. He implored me, however, not to require any one to go to that robber's nest, but to give the animals up if I didn't wish to sacrifice a man's life for them."

"And is he still abed?" asked Kohlhaas, taking off his neck-cloth.

"He's been going about in the yard again for several days now," she answered. "In short, you will see for yourself," she continued, "that it's all quite true and that this incident is merely another one of those outrages that have been committed of late against strangers at Tronka Castle."

"I must first investigate that," answered Kohlhaas. "Call him in here, Lisbeth, if he is up and about." With these words he sat down in the arm-chair and his wife, delighted at his calmness, went and fetched the groom.

"What did you do at Tronka Castle," asked Kohlhaas, as Lisbeth entered the room with him. "I am not very well pleased with you."

On the groom's pale face spots of red appeared at these words. He was silent for a while then he answered, "You are right there, Sir; for a sulphur cord, which by the will of Providence I was carrying in my pocket so as to set fire to the robber's nest from which I had been driven, I threw into the Elbe when I heard a child crying inside the castle, and I thought to myself, 'Let God's lightning burn it down; I will not!'"

Kohlhaas was disconcerted. "But for what cause were you driven from the castle?" he asked.

To this Herse answered, "Something very wrong, Sir," and wiped the perspiration from his forehead. "What is done, however, can't be undone. I wouldn't let the horses be worked to death in the fields, and so I said that they were still young and had never been in harness."

Kohlhaas, trying to hide his perplexity, answered that he had not told the exact truth, as the horses had been in harness for a little while in the early part of the previous spring. "As you were a sort of guest at the castle," he continued, "you really might have been obliging once or twice whenever they happened not to have horses enough to get the crops in as fast as they wished."

"I did so, Sir," said Herse. "I thought, as long as they looked so sulky about it, that it wouldn't hurt the blacks for once, and so on the third afternoon I hitched them in front of the others and brought in three wagonloads of grain from the fields."

Kohlhaas, whose heart was thumping, looked down at the ground and said, "They told me nothing about that, Herse!"

Herse assured him that it was so. "I wasn't disobliging save in my refusal to harness up the horses again when they had hardly eaten their fill at midday; then too, when the castellan and the steward offered to give me free fodder if I would do it, telling me to pocket the money that you had left with me to pay for feed, I answered that I would do something they didn't bargain for, turned around, and left them!"

"But surely it was not for that disobliging act that you were driven away from the castle," said Kohlhaas.

"Mercy, no!" cried the groom. "It was because of a very wicked crime! For the horses of two knights who came to the castle were put into the stable for the night and mine were tied to the stable door. And when I took the blacks from the castellan, who was putting the knights' horses into my stable, and asked where my animals were to go, he showed me a pigsty built of laths and boards against the castle wall."

"You mean," interrupted Kohlhaas, "that it was such a poor shelter for horses that it was more like a pigsty than a stable?"

"It was a pigsty, Sir," answered Herse; "really and truly a pigsty, with the pigs running in and out; I couldn't stand upright in it."

"Perhaps there was no other shelter to be found for the blacks," Kohlhaas rejoined; "and of course, in a way, the knights' horses had the right to better quarters."

"There wasn't much room," answered the groom, dropping his voice. "Counting these two, there were, in all, seven knights lodging at the castle. If it had been you, you would have had the horses moved closer together. I said I would try to rent a stable in the village, but the castellan objected that he had to keep the horses under his own eyes and told me not to dare to take them away from the courtyard."

"Hum!" said Kohlhaas. "What did you say to that?"

"As the steward said the two guests were only going to spend the night and continue on their way the next morning, I led the two horses into the pigsty. But the following day passed and they did not go, and on the third it was said the gentlemen were going to stay some weeks longer at the castle."

"After all, it was not so bad, Herse, in the pigsty, as it seemed to you when you first stuck your nose into it," said Kohlhaas.

"That's true," answered the groom. "After I had swept the place out a little, it wasn't so bad! I gave a groschen to the maid to have her put the pigs somewhere else; and by taking the boards from the roof-bars at dawn and laying them on again at night, I managed to arrange it so that the horses could stand upright in the daytime. So there they stood like geese in a coop, and stuck their heads through the roof, looking around for Kohlhaasenbrück or some other place where they would be better off."

"Well then," said Kohlhaas, "why in the world did they drive you away?"

"Sir, I'll tell you," answered the groom, "it was because they wanted to get rid of me, since, as long as I was there, they could not work the horses to death. Everywhere, in the yard, in the servants' hall, they made faces at me, and because I thought to myself, 'You can draw your jaws down until you dislocate them, for all I care,' they picked a quarrel and threw me out of the courtyard."

"But what provoked them?" cried Kohlhaas; "they must have had some sort of provocation!"

"Oh, to be sure," answered Herse; "the best imaginable! On the evening of the second day spent in the pigsty, I took the horses, which had become dirty in spite of my efforts, and started to ride them down to the horse-pond. When I reached the castle-gate and was just about to turn, I heard the castellan and the steward, with servants, dogs and cudgels, rushing out of the servants' hall after me and calling, 'Stop thief! Stop gallows-bird!' as if they were possessed. The gate-keeper stepped in front of me, and when I asked him and the raving crowd that was running at me, 'What in the world is the matter?'—'What's the matter!' answered the castellan, seizing my two black horses by the bridle. 'Where are you going with the horses?' he asked, and seized me by the chest. 'Where am I going?'

I repeated. 'Thunder and lightning! I am riding down to the horse-pond. Do you think that?'—'To the horse-pond!' cried the castellan. 'I'll teach you, you swindler, to swim along the highroad back to Kohlhaasenbrück!' And with a spiteful, vicious jerk he and the steward, who had caught me by the leg, hurled me down from the horse so that I measured my full length in the mud.

" 'Murder! Help!' I cried; 'breast straps and blankets and a bundle of linen belonging to me are in the stable.' But while the steward led the horses away, the castellan and servants fell upon me with their feet and whips and cudgels, so that I sank down behind the castle-gate half dead. And then I cried, 'The thieves! Where are they taking my horses?'—and got to my feet.—'Out of the courtyard with you!' screamed the castellan, 'Sick him, Caesar! Sick him, Hunter!' and, 'Sick him, Spitz!' he called, and a pack of more than twelve dogs rushed at me. Then I tore something from the fence, possibly a picket, and stretched out three dogs dead beside me! But when I had to give way because I was suffering from fearful wounds and bites, I heard a shrill whistle; the dogs scurried into the yard, the gates were swung shut and the bolt shot into position, and I sank down on the highroad unconscious."

Kohlhaas, white in the face, said with forced jocularity, "Didn't you really want to escape, Herse?" And as the latter, with a deep blush, looked down at the ground—"Confess to me!" said he; "You didn't like it in the pigsty; you thought to yourself, you would rather be in the stable at Kohlhaasenbrück, after all!"

"Od's thunder!"; cried Herse; "breast strap and blankets I tell you, and a bundle of linen I left behind in the pigsty. Wouldn't I have taken along three gold gulden that I had wrapped in a red silk neckcloth and hidden away behind the manger! Blazes, hell, and the devil! When you talk like that, I'd like to relight at once the sulphur cord I threw away!"

"There, there!" said the horse-dealer, "I really meant no harm. What you have said—see here, I believe it word for word, and when the matter comes up, I am ready to take the Holy Communion myself as to its truth. I am sorry that you have not fared better in my service. Go, Herse, go back to bed. Have them bring you a bottle of wine and make yourself comfortable; you shall have justice done you!" With that he stood up, made out a list of the things which the head groom had left behind in the pigsty, jotted down the value of each, asked him how high he estimated the cost of his medical treatment, and sent him from the room after shaking hands with him once more.

Thereupon he recounted to Lisbeth, his wife, the whole course of the affair, explained the true relation of events, and declared to her that he was determined to demand public justice for himself. He had the satisfaction of finding that she heartily approved his purpose, for, she said, many other travelers, perhaps less patient than he, would pass by the castle, and it was doing God's work to put a stop to disorders such as these. She added that she would manage to get together the money to pay the expenses of the lawsuit. Kohlhaas called her his brave wife, spent that day and the next very happily with her and the children, and, as soon as his business would at all permit it, set out for Dresden in order to lay his suit before the court.

Here, with the help of a lawyer whom he knew, he drew up a complaint, in which, after giving a detailed account of the outrage which Squire Wenzel Tronka had committed against him and against his groom Herse, he petitioned for the lawful punishment of the former, restoration of the horses to their original condition, and compensation for the damages which he and his groom had sustained. His case was indeed perfectly clear. The fact that the horses had been detained contrary to law threw a decisive light on everything else; and even had one been willing to assume that they had sickened by sheer accident, the demand of the horse-dealer to have them returned to him in sound condition would still have been just. While looking about him in the capital, Kohlhaas had no lack of friends, either, who promised to give his case lively support. His extensive trade in horses had secured him the acquaintance of the most important men of the country, and the honesty with which he conducted his business had won him their good will.

Kohlhaas dined cheerfully several times with his lawyer, who was himself a man of consequence, left a sum of money with him to defray the costs of the lawsuit and, fully reassured by the latter as to the outcome of the case, returned, after the lapse of some weeks, to his wife Lisbeth in Kohlhaasenbrück.

Nevertheless months passed, and the year was nearing its close before he received even a statement from Saxony concerning the suit which he had instituted there, let alone the final decree itself. After he had applied several times more to the court, he sent a confidential letter to his lawyer asking what was the cause of such undue delay. He was told in reply that the suit had been dismissed in the Dresden courts at the instance of an influential person. To the astonished reply of the horse-dealer asking what was the reason of this, the lawyer informed him that Squire Wenzel Tronka was related to two young noblemen, Hinz and Kunz Tronka, one of whom was Cup-bearer to the person of the sovereign, and the other actually Chamberlain. He also advised Kohlhaas not to make any further appeal to the court of law, but to try to regain possession of his horses which were still at Tronka Castle, giving him to understand that the Squire, who was then stopping in the capital, seemed to have ordered his people to deliver them to him. He closed with a request to excuse him from executing any further commissions in the matter, in case Kohlhaas refused to be content with this.

At this time Kohlhaas happened to be in Brandenburg, where the City Governor, Heinrich von Geusau, to whose jurisdiction Kohlhaasenbrück belonged, was busy establishing several charitable institutions for the sick and the poor out of a considerable fund which had fallen to the city. He was especially interested in fitting up, for the benefit of invalids, a mineral spring which rose in one of the villages in the vicinity, and which was thought to have greater powers than it subsequently proved to possess. As Kohlhaas had had numerous dealings with him at the time of his sojourn at Court and was therefore known to him, he allowed Herse, the head groom, who, ever since that unlucky day in Tronka Castle, had suffered pains in the chest when he breathed, to try the effect of the little healing spring, which had been inclosed and roofed over.

It so happened that the City Governor was just giving some directions, as he stood beside the depression in which Kohlhaas had placed Herse, when a messenger, whom the horse-dealer's wife had sent on after him, put in his hands the disheartening letter from his lawyer in Dresden. The City Governor, who, while speaking with the doctor, noticed that Kohlhaas let a tear fall on the letter he had just read, approached him and, in a friendly, cordial way, asked him what misfortune had befallen him. The horse-dealer handed him the letter without answering. The worthy Governor, knowing the abominable injustice done him at Tronka Castle as a result of which Herse was lying there before him sick, perhaps never to recover, clapped Kohlhaas on the shoulder and told him not to lose courage, for he would help him secure justice. In the evening, when the horse-dealer, acting upon his orders, came to the palace to see him, Kohlhaas was told that what he should do was to draw up a petition to the Elector of Brandenburg, with a short account of the incident, to inclose the lawyer's letter, and, on account of the violence which had been committed against him on Saxon territory, solicit the protection of the sovereign. He promised him to see that the petition would be delivered into the hands of the Elector together with another packet that was all ready to be dispatched; if circumstances permitted, the latter would, without fail, approach the Elector of Saxony on his behalf. Such a step would be quite sufficient to secure Kohlhaas justice at the hand of the tribunal at Dresden, in spite of the arts of the Squire and his partisans. Kohlhaas, much delighted, thanked the Governor very heartily for this new proof of his good will, and said he was only sorry that he had not instituted proceedings at once in Berlin without taking any steps in the matter at Dresden. After he had made out the complaint in due form at the office of the municipal court and delivered it to the Governor, he returned to Kohlhaasenbrück, more encouraged than ever about the outcome of his affair.

After only a few weeks, however, he was grieved to learn from a magistrate who had gone to Potsdam on business for the City Governor, that the Elector had handed the petition over to his Chancellor, Count Kallheim, and that the latter, instead of taking the course most likely to produce results and petitioning the Court at Dresden directly for investigation and punishment of the outrage, had, as a preliminary, applied to the Squire Tronka for further information.

The magistrate, who had stopped in his carriage outside of Kohlhaas' house and seemed to have been instructed to deliver this message to the horse-dealer, could give the latter no satisfactory answer to his perplexed question as to why this step had been taken. He was apparently in a hurry to continue his journey, and merely added that the Governor sent Kohlhaas word to be patient. Not until the very end of the short interview did the horse-dealer divine from some casual words he let fall, that Count Kallheim was related by marriage to the house of Tronka.

Kohlhaas, who no longer took any pleasure either in his horse-breeding, or his house or his farm, scarcely even in his wife and children, waited all the next month, full of gloomy forebodings as to the future. And, just as he had expected at the expiration of this time, Herse, somewhat benefited by the baths, came back from Brandenburg bringing a rather lengthy decree and a letter from the City Governor. The latter ran as follows: He was sorry that he could do nothing in Kohlhaas' behalf; he was sending him a decision from the Chancery of State and he advised him to fetch away the horses that he had left behind at the Tronka Castle, and then to let the matter drop.

The decree read as follows: "According to the report of the tribunal at Dresden, he was a good-for-nothing, quarrelsome person; the Squire with whom he had left the horses was not keeping them from him in any way; let him send to the castle and take them away, or at least inform the Squire where to send them to him; in any case he should not trouble the Chancery of the State with such petty quarrels and mischief-making."

Kohlhaas, who was not concerned about the horses themselves— he would have felt just as much pain if it had been a question of a couple of dogs—Kohlhaas foamed with rage when he received this letter. As often as he heard a noise in the courtyard he looked toward the gateway with the most revolting feelings of anticipation that had ever agitated his breast, to see whether the servants of the Squire had come to restore to him, perhaps even with an apology, the starved and worn-out horses. This was the only situation which he felt that his soul, well disciplined though it had been by the world, was not prepared to meet.

A short time after, however, he heard from an acquaintance who had traveled that road, that at Tronka Castle his horses were still being used for work in the fields exactly like the Squire's other horses. Through the midst of the pain caused by beholding the world in a state of such monstrous disorder, shot the inward satisfaction of knowing that from henceforth he would be at peace with himself.

He invited a bailiff, who was his neighbor, to come to see him. The latter had long cherished the idea of enlarging his estate by purchasing the property which adjoined it. When he had seated himself Kohlhaas asked him how much he would give for his possessions on Brandenburg and Saxon territory, for house and farm, in a lump, immovable or not.

Lisbeth, his wife, grew pale when she heard his words. She turned around and picked up her youngest child who was playing on the floor behind her. While the child pulled at her kerchief, she darted glances of mortal terror past the little one's red cheeks, at the horse-dealer, and at a paper which he held in his hand.

The bailiff stared at his neighbor in astonishment and asked him what had suddenly given him such strange ideas; to which the horse-dealer, with as much gaiety as he could muster, replied that the idea of selling his farm on the banks of the Havel was not an entirely new one, but that they had often before discussed the subject together. As for his house in the outskirts of Dresden—in comparison with the farm it was only a tag end and need not be taken into consideration. In short, if the bailiff would do as he wished and take over both pieces of property, he was ready to close the contract with him. He added with rather forced pleasantry that Kohlhaasenbrück was not the world; that there might be objects in life compared with which that of taking care of his home and family as a father is supposed to would be a secondary and unworthy one. In a word, he must tell him that his soul was intent upon accomplishing great things, of which, perhaps, he would hear shortly. The bailiff, reassured by these words, said jokingly to Kohlhaas' wife, who was kissing her child repeatedly, " Surely he will not insist upon being paid immediately!" Then he laid his hat and cane, which he had been holding between his knees, on the table, and taking the paper, which the horse-dealer was holding in his hand, began to read. Kohlhaas, moving closer to him, explained that it was a contingent contract to purchase, drawn up by himself, his right to cancel the contract expiring in four weeks. He showed the bailiff that nothing was wanting but the signatures, the insertion of the purchase-price itself, and the amount of the forfeit that he, Kohlhaas, would agree to pay in case he should withdraw from the contract within the four weeks' time. Again Kohlhaas gaily urged his friend to make an offer, assuring him that he would be reasonable and would make the conditions easy for him. His wife was walking up and down the room; she breathed so hard that the kerchief, at which the boy had been pulling, threatened to fall clear off her shoulder. The bailiff said that he really had no way of judging the value of the property in Dresden; whereupon Kohlhaas, shoving toward him some letters which had been exchanged at the time of its purchase, answered that he estimated it at one hundred gold gulden, although the letters would show that it had cost him almost half as much again. The bailiff who, on reading the deed of sale, found that, strangely enough, he too was guaranteed the privilege of withdrawing from the bargain, had already half made up his mind; but he said that, of course, he could make no use of the stud-horses which were in the stables. When Kohlhaas replied that he wasn't at all inclined to part with the horses either, and that he also desired to keep for himself some weapons which were hanging in the armory, the bailiff still continued to hesitate for some time. At last he repeated an offer that, once before, when they were out walking together, he had made him, half in jest and half in earnest—a trifling offer indeed, in comparison with the value of the property. Kohlhaas pushed the pen and ink over for him to sign, and when the bailiff, who could not believe his senses, again inquired if he were really in earnest, and the horse-dealer asked, a little sensitively, whether he thought that he was only jesting with him, then took up the pen, though with a very serious face, and wrote. However, he crossed out the clause concerning the sum to be forfeited in case the seller should repent of the transaction, bound himself to a loan of one hundred gold gulden on a mortgage on the Dresden property, which he absolutely refused to buy outright, and allowed Kohlhaas full liberty to withdraw from the transaction at any time within two months.

The horse-dealer, touched by this conduct, shook his hand with great cordiality, and after they had furthermore agreed on the principal conditions, to the effect that a fourth part of the purchase-price should without fail be paid immediately in cash, and the balance paid into the Hamburg bank in three months' time, Kohlhaas called for wine in order to celebrate such a happy conclusion of the bargain. He told the maid-servant who entered with the bottles, to order Sternbald, the groom, to saddle the chestnut horse for him, as he had to ride to the capital, where he had some business to attend to. He gave them to understand that, in a short time, when he returned, he would talk more frankly concerning what he must for the present continue to keep to himself. As he poured out the wine into the glasses, he asked about the Poles and the Turks who were just then at war, and involved the bailiff in many political conjectures on the subject; then, after finally drinking once more to the success of their business, he allowed the latter to depart.

When the bailiff had left the room, Lisbeth fell down on her knees before her husband. "If you have any affection for me," she cried, "and for the children whom I have borne you; if you have not already, for what reason I know not, cast us out from your heart, then tell me what these horrible preparations mean!"

Kohlhaas answered, "Dearest wife, they mean nothing which need cause you any alarm, as matters stand at present. I have received a decree in which I am told that my complaint against the Squire Wenzel Tronka is a piece of impertinent mischief-making. As there must exist some misunderstanding in this matter, I have made up my mind to present my complaint once more, this time in person, to the sovereign himself."

"But why will you sell your house?" she cried, rising with a look of despair.

The horse-dealer, clasping her tenderly to his breast, answered, "Because, dear Lisbeth, I do not care to remain in a country where they will not protect me in my rights. If I am to be kicked I would rather be a dog than a man! I am sure that my wife thinks about this just as I do."

"How do you know," she asked wildly, "that they will not protect you in your rights? If, as is becoming, you approach the Elector humbly with your petition, how do you know that it will be thrown aside or answered by a refusal to listen to you!"

"Very well!" answered Kohlhaas; "my fears on the subject are unfounded, my house isn't sold yet, either. The Elector himself is just, I know, and if I can only succeed in getting past those who surround him and in reaching his person, I do not doubt that I shall secure justice, and that, before the week is out, I shall return joyfully home again to you and my old trade. In that case I would gladly stay with you," he added, kissing her, "until the end of my life! But it is advisable," he continued, "to be prepared for any emergency, and for that reason I should like you, if it is possible, to go away for a while with the children to your aunt in Schwerin, whom, moreover, you have, for some time, been intending to visit!"

"What!" cried the housewife; "I am to go to Schwerin to go across the frontier with the children to my aunt in Schwerin?" Terror choked her words.

"Certainly," answered Kohlhaas, "and, if possible, right away, so that I may not be hindered by any family considerations in the steps I intend to take in my suit."

"Oh, I understand you!" she cried. "You now need nothing but weapons and horses; whoever will may take everything else!" With this she turned away and, in tears, flung herself down on a chair.

Kohlhaas exclaimed in alarm, "Dearest Lisbeth, what are you doing! God has blessed me with wife and children and worldly goods; am I today for the first time to wish that it were otherwise?" He sat down gently beside his wife, who at these words had flushed up and fallen on his neck. "Tell me!" said he, smoothing the curls away from her forehead. "What shall I do? Shall I give up my case? Do you wish me to go to Tronka Castle, beg the knight to restore the horses to me, mount and ride them back home?"

Lisbeth did not dare to cry out, "Yes, yes, yes!" She shook her head, weeping, and, clasping him close, kissed him passionately.

"Well, then," cried Kohlhaas, "if you feel that, in case I am to continue my trade, justice must be done me, do not deny me the liberty which I must have in order to procure it!"

With that he stood up and said to the groom who had come to tell him that the chestnut horse was saddled, "tomorrow the bay horses must be harnessed up to take my wife to Schwerin." Lisbeth said that she had an idea! She rose, wiped the tears from her eyes, and, going over to the desk where he had seated himself, asked him if he would give her the petition and let her go to Berlin in his stead and hand it to the Elector. For more reasons than one Kohlhaas was deeply moved by this change of attitude. He drew her down on his lap, and said, " Dearest wife, that is hardly practicable. The sovereign is surrounded by a great many people; whoever wishes to approach him is exposed to many annoyances."

Lisbeth rejoined that, in a thousand cases, it was easier for a woman to approach him than it was for a man. "Give me the petition," she repeated, "and if all that you wish is the assurance that it shall reach his hands, I vouch for it; he shall receive it!"

Kohlhaas, who had had many proofs of her courage as well as of her wisdom, asked her how she intended to go about it. To this she answered, looking shamefacedly at the ground, that the castellan of the Elector's palace had paid court to her in former days, when he had been in service in Schwerin; that, to be sure, he was married now and had several children, but that she was not yet entirely forgotten, and, in short, her husband should leave it to her to take advantage of this circumstance as well as of many others which it would require too much time to enumerate. Kohlhaas kissed her joyfully, said that he accepted her proposal, and informed her that for her to lodge with the wife of the castellan would be all that was necessary to enable her to approach the sovereign inside the palace itself. Then he gave her the petition, had the bay horses harnessed, and sent her off, well bundled up, accompanied by Sternbald, his faithful groom.

Of all the unsuccessful steps, however, which he had taken in regard to his suit, this journey was the most unfortunate. For only a few days later Sternbald entered the courtyard again, leading the horses at a walk before the wagon, in which lay his wife, stretched out, with a dangerous contusion of the chest. Kohlhaas, who approached the wagon with a white face, could learn nothing coherent concerning the cause of the accident. The castellan, the groom said, had not been at home; they had therefore been obliged to put up at an inn that stood near the palace. Lisbeth had left this inn on the following morning, ordering the servant to stay behind with the horses; not until evening had she returned, and then only in this condition. It seemed she had pressed forward too boldly toward the person of the sovereign, and without any fault of his, but merely through the rough zeal of a body-guard which surrounded him, she had received a blow on the chest with the shaft of a lance. At least this was what the people said who, toward evening, had brought her back unconscious to the inn; for she herself could talk but little for the blood which flowed from her mouth. The petition had been taken from her afterward by a knight. Sternbald said that it had been his wish to jump on a horse at once and bring the news of the unfortunate accident to his master, but, in spite of the remonstrances of the surgeon who had been called in, she had insisted on being taken back to her husband at Kohlhaasenbrück without previously sending him word. She was completely exhausted by the journey and Kohlhaas put her to bed, where she lived a few days longer, struggling painfully to draw breath.

They tried in vain to restore her to consciousness in order to learn the particulars of what had occurred; she lay with fixed, already glassy eyes, and gave no answer.

Once only, shortly before her death, did she recover consciousness. A minister of the Lutheran church (which religion, then in its infancy, she had embraced, following the example of her husband) was standing beside her bed, reading in a loud solemn voice, full of emotion, a chapter of the Bible, when she suddenly looked up at him with a stern expression, and, taking the Bible out of his hand, as though there were no need to read to her from it, turned over the leaves for some time and seemed to be searching for some special passage. At last, with her fore-finger she pointed out to Kohlhaas, who was sitting beside her bed, the verse: "Forgive your enemies; do good to them that hate you." As she did so she pressed his hand with a look full of deep and tender feeling, and passed away.

Kohlhaas thought, "May God—never forgive me the way I forgive the Squire!" Then he kissed her amid freely flowing tears, closed her eyes, and left the chamber.

He took the hundred gold gulden which the bailiff had already sent him for the stables in Dresden, and ordered a funeral ceremony that seemed more suitable for a princess than for her—an oaken coffin heavily trimmed with metal, cushions of silk with gold and silver tassels, and a grave eight yards deep lined with stones and mortar. He himself stood beside the vault with his youngest child in his arms and watched the work. On the day of the funeral the corpse, white as snow, was placed in a room which he had had draped with black cloth.

The minister had just completed a touching address by the side of the bier when the sovereign's answer to the petition which the dead woman had presented was delivered to Kohlhaas. By this decree he was ordered to fetch the horses from Tronka Castle and, under pain of imprisonment, not to bring any further action in the matter. Kohlhaas put the letter in his pocket and had the coffin carried out to the hearse.

As soon as the mound had been raised, the cross planted on it, and the guests who had been present at the interment had taken their departure, Kohlhaas flung himself down once more before his wife's empty bed, and then set about the business of revenge.

He sat down and made out a decree in which, by virtue of his own innate authority, he condemned the Squire Wenzel Tronka within the space of three days after sight to lead back to Kohlhaasenbrück the two black horses which he had taken from him and overworked in the fields, and with his own hands to feed the horses in Kohlhaas' stables until they were fat again. This decree he sent off to the Squire by a mounted messenger, and instructed the latter to return to Kohlhaasenbrück as soon as he had delivered the document.

As the three days went by without the horses being returned, Kohlhaas called Herse and informed him of what he had ordered the Squire to do in regard to fattening them. Then he asked Herse two questions: first, whether he would ride with him to Tronka Castle and fetch the Squire; and, secondly, whether Herse would be willing to apply the whip to the young gentleman after he had been brought to the stables at Kohlhaasenbrück, in case he should be remiss in carrying out the conditions of the decree. As soon as Herse understood what was meant he shouted joyfully—"Sir, this very day!" and, throwing his hat into the air, he cried that he was going to have a thong with ten knots plaited in order to teach the Squire how to curry-comb. After this Kohlhaas sold the house, packed the children into a wagon, and sent them over the border. When darkness fell he called the other servants together, seven in number, and every one of them true as gold to him, armed them and provided them with mounts and set out for the Tronka Castle.

At night-fall of the third day, with this little troop he rode down the toll-gatherer and the gate-keeper who were standing in conversation in the arched gateway, and attacked the castle. They set fire to all the outbuildings in the castle inclosure, and, while, amid the outburst of the flames, Herse hurried up the winding staircase into the tower of the castellan's quarters, and with blows and stabs fell upon the castellan and the steward who were sitting, half dressed, over the cards, Kohlhaas at the same time dashed into the castle in search of the Squire Wenzel. Thus it is that the angel of judgment descends from heaven; the Squire, who, to the accompaniment of immoderate laughter, was just reading aloud to a crowd of young friends the decree which the horse-dealer had sent to him, had no sooner heard the sound of his voice in the courtyard than, turning suddenly pale as death, he cried out to the gentlemen—"Brothers, save yourselves!" and disappeared. As Kohlhaas entered the room he seized by the shoulders a certain Squire, Hans Tronka, who came at him, and flung him into the corner of the room with such force that his brains spurted out over the stone floor. While the other knights, who had drawn their weapons, were being overpowered and scattered by the grooms, Kohlhaas asked where the Squire Wenzel Tronka was. Realizing the ignorance of the stunned men, he kicked open the doors of two apartments leading into the wings of the castle and, after searching in every direction throughout the rambling building and finding no one, he went down, cursing, into the castle yard, in order to place guards at the exits.

In the meantime, from the castle and the wings, which had caught fire from the out-buildings, thick columns of smoke were rising heavenward. While Sternbald and three busy grooms were gathering together everything in the castle that was not fastened securely and throwing it down among the horses as fair spoils, from the open windows of the castellan's quarters the corpses of the castellan and the steward, with their wives and children, were flung down into the courtyard amid the joyful shouts of Herse. As Kohlhaas descended the steps of the castle, the gouty old housekeeper who managed the Squire's establishment threw herself at his feet. Pausing on the step, he asked her where the Squire Wenzel Tronka was. She answered in a faint trembling voice that she thought he had taken refuge in the chapel. Kohlhaas then called two men with torches, and, since they had no keys, he had the door broken open with crowbars and axes. He knocked over altars and pews; nevertheless, to his anger and grief, he did not find the Squire.

It happened that, at the moment when Kohlhaas came out of the chapel, a young servant, one of the retainers of the castle, came hurrying upon his way to get the Squire's chargers out of a large stone stable which was threatened by the flames. Kohlhaas, who at that very moment spied his two blacks in a little shed roofed with straw, asked the man why he did not rescue the two blacks. The latter, sticking the key in the stable-door, answered that he surely must see that the shed was already in flames. Kohlhaas tore the key violently from the stable-door, threw it over the wall, and, raining blows as thick as hail on the man with the flat of his sword, drove him into the burning shed and, amid the horrible laughter of the bystanders, forced him to rescue the black horses. Nevertheless, when the man, pale with fright, reappeared with the horses, only a few moments before the shed fell in behind him, he no longer found Kohlhaas. Betaking himself to the men gathered in the castle inclosure, he asked the horse-dealer, who several times turned his back on him, what he was to do with the animals now.

Kohlhaas suddenly raised his foot with such terrible force that the kick, had it landed, would have meant death; then, without answering, he mounted his bay horse, stationed himself under the gateway of the castle, and, while his men continued their work of destruction, silently awaited the break of day.

When the morning dawned the entire castle had burned down and only the walls remained standing; no one was left in it but Kohlhaas and his seven men. He dismounted from his horse and, in the bright sunlight which illuminated every crack and corner, once more searched the inclosure. When he had to admit, hard though it was for him to do so, that the expedition against the castle had failed, with a heart full of pain and grief he sent Herse and some of the other men to gather news of the direction in which the Squire had fled. He felt especially troubled about a rich nunnery for ladies of rank, Erlabrunn by name, which was situated on the shores of the Mulde, and whose abbess, Antonia Tronka, was celebrated in the neighborhood as a pious, charitable, and saintly woman. The unhappy Kohlhaas thought it only too probable that the Squire, stripped as he was of all necessities, had taken refuge in this nunnery, since the abbess was his own aunt and had been his governess in his early childhood. After informing himself of these particulars, Kohlhaas ascended the tower of the castellan's quarters in the interior of which there was still a habitable room, and there he drew up a so-called "Kohlhaas mandate" in which he warned the country not to offer assistance to Squire Wenzel Tronka, against whom he was waging just warfare, and, furthermore, commanded every inhabitant, instead, relatives and friends not excepted, to surrender him under penalty of death and the inevitable burning down of everything that might be called property.

This declaration he scattered broadcast in the surrounding country through travelers and strangers; he even went so far as to give Waldmann, his servant, a copy of it, with definite instructions to carry it to Erlabrunn and place it in the hands of Lady Antonia. Thereupon he had a talk with some of the servants of Tronka Castle who were dissatisfied with the Squire and, attracted by the prospect of plunder, wished to enter the horse-dealer's service. He armed them after the manner of foot-soldiers, with cross-bows and daggers, taught them how to mount behind the men on horseback, and after he had turned into money everything that the company had collected and had distributed it among them, he spent some hours in the gateway of the castle, resting after his sorry labor.

Toward midday Herse came and confirmed what Kohlhaas' heart, which was always filled with the most gloomy forebodings, had already told him—namely, that the Squire was then in the nunnery of Erlabrunn with the old Lady Antonia Tronka, his aunt. It seemed that, through a door in the rear wall behind the castle, leading into the open air, he had escaped down a narrow stone stairway which, protected by a little roof, ran down to a few boats on the Elbe. At least, Herse reported that at midnight the Squire in a skiff without rudder or oars had arrived at a village on the Elbe, to the great astonishment of the inhabitants who were assembled on account of the fire at Tronka Castle and that he had gone on toward Erlabrunn in a village cart.

Kohlhaas sighed deeply at this news; he asked whether the horses had been fed, and when they answered "Yes," he had his men mount, and in three hours' time he was at the gates of Erlabrunn. Amid the rumbling of a distant storm on the horizon, he and his troop entered the courtyard of the convent with torches which they had lighted before reaching the spot. Just as Waldmann, his servant, came forward to announce that the mandate had been duly delivered, Kohlhaas saw the abbess and the chapter-warden step out under the portal of the nunnery, engaged in agitated conversation. While the chapter-warden, a little old man with snow-white hair, shooting furious glances at Kohlhaas, was having his armor put on and, in a bold voice, called to the men-servants surrounding him to ring the storm-bell, the abbess, white as a sheet, and holding the silver image of the Crucified One in her hand, descended the sloping driveway and, with all her nuns, flung herself down before Kohlhaas' horse.

Herse and Sternbald overpowered the chapter-warden, who had no sword in his hand, and led him off as a prisoner among the horses, while Kohlhaas asked the abbess where Squire Wenzel Tronka was. She unfastened from her girdle a large ring of keys, and answered, "In Wittenberg, Kohlhaas, worthy man!"— adding, in a shaking voice, "Fear God, and do no wrong!" Kohlhaas, plunged back into the hell of unsatisfied thirst for revenge, wheeled his horse and was about to cry, "Set fire to the buildings!" when a terrific thunder-bolt struck close beside him. Turning his horse around again toward the abbess he asked her whether she had received his mandate. The lady answered in a weak, scarcely audible voice—"Just a few moments ago!"—"When?"—"Two hours after the Squire, my nephew, had taken his departure, as truly as God is my help!" When Waldmann, the groom, to whom Kohlhaas turned with a lowering glance, stammered out a confirmation of this fact, saying that the waters of the Mulde, swollen by the rain, had prevented his arriving until a few moments ago, Kohlhaas came to his senses. A sudden, terrible downpour of rain, sweeping across the pavement of the courtyard and extinguishing the torches, relaxed the tension of the unhappy man's grief; doffing his hat curtly to the abbess, he wheeled his horse, dug in his spurs, calling "Follow me, my brothers; the Squire is in Wittenberg," and left the nunnery.

The night having set in, he stopped at an inn on the highroad, and had to rest here for a day because the horses were so exhausted. As he clearly saw that with a troop of ten men (for his company numbered that many now) he could not defy a place like Wittenberg, he drew up a second mandate, in which, after a short account of what had happened to him in the land, he summoned "every good Christian," as he expressed it, to whom he "solemnly promised bounty-money and other perquisites of war, to take up his quarrel against Squire Tronka as the common enemy of all Christians." In another mandate which appeared shortly after this he called himself "a free gentleman of the Empire and of the World, subject only to God"— an example of morbid and misplaced fanaticism which, nevertheless, with the sound of his money and the prospect of plunder, procured him a crowd of recruits from among the rabble, whom the peace with Poland had deprived of a livelihood. In fact, he had thirty-odd men when he crossed back to the right side of the Elbe, bent upon reducing Wittenberg to ashes.

He encamped with horses and men in an old tumble-down brick-kiln, in the solitude of a dense forest which surrounded the town at that time. No sooner had Sternbald, whom he had sent in disguise into the city with the mandate, brought him word that it was already known there, than he set out with his troop on the eve of Whitsuntide; and while the citizens lay sound asleep, he set the town on fire at several points simultaneously. At the same time, while his men were plundering the suburbs, he fastened a paper to the door-post of a church to the effect that "he, Kohlhaas, had set the city on fire, and if the Squire were not delivered to him he would burn down the city so completely that," as he expressed it, "he would not need to look behind any wall to find him."

The terror of the citizens at such an unheard-of outrage was indescribable, though, as it was fortunately a rather calm summer night, the flames had not destroyed more than nineteen buildings, among which, however, was a church. Toward daybreak, as soon as the fire had been partially extinguished, the aged Governor of the province, Otto von Gorgas, sent out immediately a company of fifty men to capture the bloodthirsty madman. The captain in command of the company, Gerstenberg by name, bore himself so badly, however, that the whole expedition, instead of subduing Kohlhaas, rather helped him to a most dangerous military reputation. For the captain separated his men into several divisions, with the intention of surrounding and crushing Kohlhaas; but the latter, holding his troop together, attacked and beat him at isolated points, so that by the evening of the following day, not a single man of the whole company in which the hopes of the country were centred, remained in the field against him. Kohlhaas, who had lost some of his men in these fights, again set fire to the city on the morning of the next day, and his murderous measures were so well taken that once more a number of houses and almost all the barns in the suburbs were burned down. At the same time he again posted the well-known mandate, this time, furthermore, on the corners of the city hall itself, and he added a notice concerning the fate of Captain von Gerstenberg who had been sent against him by the Governor, and whom he had overwhelmingly defeated.

The Governor of the province, highly incensed at this defiance, placed himself with several knights at the head of a troop of one hundred and fifty men. At a written request he gave Squire Wenzel Tronka a guard to protect him from the violence of the people, who flatly insisted that he must be removed from the city. After the Governor had had guards placed in all the villages in the vicinity, and also had sentinels stationed on the city walls to prevent a surprise, he himself set out on Saint Gervaise's day to capture the dragon who was devastating the land. The horse-dealer was clever enough to keep out of the way of this troop. By skilfully executed marches he enticed the Governor five leagues away from the city, and by means of various manœuvres he gave the other the mistaken notion that, hard pressed by superior numbers, he was going to throw himself into Brandenburg. Then, when the third night closed in, he made a forced ride back to Wittenberg, and for the third time set fire to the city. Herse, who crept into the town in disguise, carried out this horrible feat of daring, and because of a sharp north wind that was blowing, the fire proved so destructive and spread so rapidly that in less than three hours forty-two houses, two churches, several convents and schools, and the very residence of the electoral governor of the province were reduced to ruins and ashes.

The Governor who, when the day broke, believed his adversary to be in Brandenburg, returned by forced marches when informed of what had happened, and found the city in a general uproar. The people were massed by thousands around the Squire's house, which was barricaded with heavy timbers and posts, and with wild cries they demanded his expulsion from the city. Two burgomasters, Jenkens and Otto by name, who were present in their official dress at the head of the entire city council, tried in vain to explain that they absolutely must await the return of a courier who had been dispatched to the President of the Chancery of State for permission to send the Squire to Dresden, whither he himself, for many reasons, wished to go. The unreasoning crowd, armed with pikes and staves, cared nothing for these words. After handling rather roughly some councilors who were insisting upon the adoption of vigorous measures, the mob was about to storm the house where the Squire was and level it to the ground, when the Governor, Otto von Gorgas, appeared in the city at the head of his troopers. This worthy gentleman, who was wont by his mere presence to inspire people to respectful obedience, had, as though in compensation for the failure of the expedition from which he was returning, succeeded in taking prisoner three stray members of the incendiary's band, right in front of the gates of the city. While the prisoners were being loaded with chains before the eyes of the people, he made a clever speech to the city councilors, assuring them that he was on Kohlhaas' track and thought that he would soon be able to bring the incendiary himself in chains. By force of all these reassuring circumstances he succeeded in allaying the fears of the assembled crowd and in partially reconciling them to the presence of the Squire until the return of the courier from Dresden. He dismounted from his horse and, accompanied by some knights, entered the house after the posts and stockades had been cleared away. He found the Squire, who was falling from one faint into another, in the hands of two doctors, who with essences and stimulants were trying to restore him to consciousness. As Sir Otto von Gorgas realized that this was not the moment to exchange any words with him on the subject of the behavior of which he had been guilty, he merely told him, with a look of quiet contempt, to dress himself, and, for his own safety, to follow him to the apartments of the knight's prison. They put a doublet and a helmet on the Squire and when, with chest half bare on account of the difficulty he had in breathing, he appeared in the street on the arm of the Governor and his brother-in-law, the Count of Gerschau, blasphemous and horrible curses against him rose to heaven. The mob, whom the lansquenets found it very difficult to restrain, called him a bloodsucker, a miserable public pest and a tormentor of men, the curse of the city of Wittenberg, and the ruin of Saxony. After a wretched march through the devastated city, in the course of which the Squire's helmet fell off several times without his missing it and had to be replaced on his head by the knight who was behind him, they reached the prison at last, where he disappeared into a tower under the protection of a strong guard. Meanwhile the return of the courier with the decree of the Elector had aroused fresh alarm in the city. For the Saxon government, to which the citizens of Dresden had made direct application in an urgent petition, refused to permit the Squire to sojourn in the electoral capital before the incendiary had been captured. The Governor was instructed rather to use all the power at his command to protect the Squire just where he was, since he had to stay somewhere, but in order to pacify the good city of Wittenberg, the inhabitants were informed that a force of five hundred men under the command of Prince Friedrich of Meissen was already on the way to protect them from further molestation on the part of Kohlhaas.

The Governor saw clearly that a decree of this kind was wholly inadequate to pacify the people. For not only had several small advantages gained by the horse-dealer in skirmishes outside the city sufficed to spread extremely disquieting rumors as to the size to which his band had grown; his way of waging warfare with ruffians in disguise who slunk about under cover of darkness with pitch, straw, and sulphur, unheard of and quite without precedent as it was, would have rendered ineffectual an even larger protecting force than the one which was advancing under the Prince of Meissen. After reflecting a short time, the Governor determined therefore to suppress altogether the decree he had received; he merely posted at all the street corners a letter from the Prince of Meissen, announcing his arrival. At daybreak a covered wagon left the courtyard of the knight's prison and took the road to Leipzig, accompanied by four heavily armed troopers who, in an indefinite sort of way, let it be understood that they were bound for the Pleissenburg. The people having thus been satisfied on the subject of the ill-starred Squire, whose existence seemed identified with fire and sword, the Governor himself set out with a force of three hundred men to join Prince Friedrich of Meissen. In the mean time Kohlhaas, thanks to the strange position which he had assumed in the world, had in truth increased the numbers of his band to one hundred and nine men, and he had also collected in Jessen a store of weapons with which he had fully armed them. When informed of the two tempests that were sweeping down upon him, he decided to go to meet them with the speed of the hurricane before they should join to overwhelm him. In accordance with this plan he attacked the Prince of Meissen the very next night, surprising him near Mühlberg. In this fight, to be sure, he was greatly grieved to lose Herse, who was struck down at his side by the first shots but, embittered by this loss, in a three-hour battle he so roughly handled the Prince of Meissen, who was unable to collect his forces in the town, that at break of day the latter was obliged to take the road back to Dresden, owing to several severe wounds which he had received and the complete disorder into which his troops had been thrown. Kohlhaas, made foolhardy by this victory, turned back to attack the Governor before the latter could learn of it, fell upon him at midday in the open country near the village of Damerow, and fought him until nightfall, with murderous losses, to be sure, but with corresponding success. Indeed, the next morning he would certainly with the remnant of his band have renewed the attack on the Governor, who had thrown himself into the churchyard at Damerow, if the latter had not received through spies the news of the defeat of the Prince at Mühlberg and therefore deemed it wiser to return to Wittenberg to await a more propitious moment.

Five days after the dispersion of these two bodies of troops, Kohlhaas arrived before Leipzig and set fire to the city on three different sides. In the mandate which he scattered broadcast on this occasion he called himself "a vicegerent of the archangel Michael who had come to visit upon all who, in this controversy, should take the part of the Squire, punishment by fire and sword for the villainy into which the whole world was plunged." At the same time, having surprised the castle at Lützen and fortified himself in it, he summoned the people to join him and help establish a better order of things. With a sort of insane fanaticism the mandate was signed: "Done at the seat of our provisional world government, our ancient castle at Lützen."

As the good fortune of the inhabitants of Leipzig would have it, the fire, owing to a steady rain which was falling, did not spread, so that, thanks to the rapid action of the means at hand for extinguishing fires, only a few small shops which lay around the Pleissenburg went up in flames; nevertheless the presence of the desperate incendiary, and his erroneous impression that the Squire was in Leipzig, caused unspeakable consternation in the city. When a troop of one hundred and eighty men at arms that had been sent against him returned defeated, nothing else remained for the city councilors, who did not wish to jeopardize the wealth of the place, but to bar the gates completely and set the citizens to keep watch day and night outside the walls. In vain the city council had declarations posted in the villages of the surrounding country, with the positive assurance that the Squire was not in the Pleissenburg. The horse-dealer, in similar manifestos, insisted that he was in the Pleissenburg and declared that if the Squire were not there, he, Kohlhaas, would at any rate proceed as though he were until he should have been told the name of the place where his enemy was to be found. The Elector, notified by courier of the straits to which the city of Leipzig was reduced, declared that he was already gathering a force of two thousand men and would put himself at their head in order to capture Kohlhaas. He administered to Sir Otto von Gorgas a severe rebuke for the misleading and ill-considered artifice to which he had resorted to rid the vicinity of Wittenberg of the incendiary. Nor can any one describe the confusion which seized all Saxony, and especially the electoral capital, when it was learned there that in all the villages near Leipzig a declaration addressed to Kohlhaas had been placarded, no one knew by whom, to the effect that "Wenzel, the Squire, was with his cousins Hinz and Kunz in Dresden."

It was under these circumstances that Doctor Martin Luther, supported by the authority which his position in the world gave him, undertook the task of forcing Kohlhaas, by the power of kindly words, back within the limits set by the social order of the day. Building upon an element of good in the breast of the incendiary, he had posted in all the cities and market-towns of the Electorate a placard addressed to him, which read as follows:

"Kohlhaas, thou who claimest to be sent to wield the sword of justice, what is it that thou, presumptuous man, art making bold to attempt in the madness of thy stoneblind passion—thou who art filled from head to foot with injustice? Because the sovereign, to whom thou art subject, has denied thee thy rights—thy rights in the struggle for a paltry trifle—thou arisest, godless man, with fire and sword, and like a wolf of the wilderness dost burst upon the peaceful community which he protects. Thou, who misleadest men with this declaration full of untruthfulness and guile, dost thou think, sinner, to satisfy God therewith in that future day which shall shine into the recesses of every heart? How canst thou say that thy rights have been denied thee—thou, whose savage breast, animated by the inordinate desire for base revenge, completely gave up the endeavor to procure justice after the first half-hearted attempts, which came to naught? Is a bench full of constables and beadles who suppress a letter that is presented, or who withhold a judgment that they should deliver—is this thy supreme authority? And must I tell thee, impious man, that the supreme authority of the land knows nothing whatever about thine affair—nay, more, that the sovereign against whom thou art rebelling does not even know thy name, so that when thou shalt one day come before the throne of God thinking to accuse him, he will be able to say with a serene countenance, 'I have done no wrong to this man, Lord, for my soul is ignorant of his existence.' Know that the sword which thou wieldest is the sword of robbery and bloodthirstiness. A rebel art thou, and no warrior of the righteous God; wheel and gallows are thy goal on earth—gallows and, in the life to come, damnation which is ordained for crime and godlessness.

Wittenberg, etc.
Martin Luther."

When Sternbald and Waldmann, to their great consternation, discovered the placard which had been affixed to the gateway of the castle at Lützen during the night, Kohlhaas within the castle was just revolving in his distracted mind a new plan for the burning of Leipzig—for he placed no faith in the notices posted in the villages announcing that Squire Wenzel was in Dresden, since they were not signed by any one, let alone by the municipal council, as he had required. For several days the two men hoped in vain that Kohlhaas would perceive Luther's placard, for they did not care to approach him on the subject. Gloomy and absorbed in thought, he did indeed, in the evening, appear, but only to give his brief commands, and he noticed nothing. Finally one morning, when he was about to have two of his followers strung up for plundering in the vicinity against his express orders, Sternbald and Waldmann determined to call his attention to it. With the pomp which he had adopted since his last manifesto—a large cherubim's sword on a red leather cushion, ornamented with golden tassels, borne before him, and twelve men with burning torches following him—Kohlhaas was just returning from the place of execution, while the people on both sides timidly made way for him. At that moment the two men, with their swords under their arms, walked, in a way that could not fail to excite his surprise, around the pillar to which the placard was attached.

When Kohlhaas, sunk in thought and with his hands folded behind his back, came under the portal, he raised his eyes and started back in surprise, and as the two men at sight of him drew back respectfully, he advanced with rapid steps to the pillar, watching them absent-mindedly. But who can describe the storm of emotion in his soul when he beheld there the paper accusing him of injustice, signed by the most beloved and honored name he knew—the name of Martin Luther! A dark flush spread over his face; taking off his helmet he read the document through twice from beginning to end, then walked back among his men with irresolute glances as though he were about to speak, yet said nothing. He unfastened the paper from the pillar, read it through once again, and cried, "Waldmann! have my horse saddled!"—then, "Sternbald, follow me into the castle!" and with that he disappeared. It had needed but these few words of that godly man to disarm him suddenly in the midst of all the dire destruction that he was plotting.

He threw on the disguise of a Thuringian farmer and told Sternbald that a matter of the greatest importance obliged him to go to

Wittenberg. In the presence of some of his most trustworthy men he turned over to Sternbald the command of the band remaining in Lützen, and with the assurance that he would be back in three days, during which time no attack was to be feared, he departed for Wittenberg. He put up at an inn under an assumed name, and at nightfall, wrapped in his cloak and provided with a brace of pistols which he had taken at the sack of Tronka Castle, entered Luther's room. When Luther, who was sitting at his desk with a mass of books and papers before him, saw the extraordinary stranger enter his room and bolt the door behind him, he asked who he was and what he wanted. The man, who was holding his hat respectfully in his hand, had no sooner, with a diffident presentiment of the terror that he would cause, made answer that he was Michael Kohlhaas, the horse-dealer, than Luther cried out, "Stand far back from me!" and rising from the desk added, as he hurried toward a bell, "Your breath is pestilence, your presence destruction!"

Without stirring from the spot Kohlhaas drew his pistol and said, "Most reverend Sir, if you touch the bell this pistol will stretch me lifeless at your feet! Sit down and hear me. You are not safer among the angels, whose psalms you are writing down, than you are with me."

Luther sat down and asked, "What do you want!" Kohlhaas answered, "I wish to refute the opinion you have of me, that I am an unjust man! You told me in your placard that my sovereign knows nothing about my case. Very well; procure me a safe-conduct and I will go to Dresden and lay it before him."

"Impious and terrible man!" cried Luther, puzzled and, at the same time, reassured by these words. "Who gave you the right to attack Squire Tronka in pursuance of a decree issued on your own authority, and, when you did not find him in his castle, to visit with fire and sword the whole community which protects him?"

Kohlhaas answered, "Reverend Sir, no one, henceforth. Information which I received from Dresden deceived and misled me! The war which I am waging against society is a crime, so long as I haven't been cast out—and you have assured me that I have not."

"Cast out!" cried Luther, looking at him. "What mad thoughts have taken possession of you? Who could have cast you out from the community of the state in which you lived? Indeed where, as long as states have existed, has there ever been a case of any one, no matter who, being cast out of such a community!"

"I call that man cast out," answered Kohlhaas, clenching his fist, "who is denied the protection of the laws. For I need this protection, if my peaceable business is to prosper. Yes, it is for this that, with all my possessions, I take refuge in this community, and he who denies me this protection casts me out among the savages of the desert; he places in my hand—how can you try to deny it?—the club with which to protect myself."

"Who has denied you the protection of the laws?" cried Luther. "Did I not write you that your sovereign, to whom you addressed your complaint, has never heard of it? If state-servants behind his back suppress lawsuits or otherwise trifle with his sacred name without his knowledge, who but God has the right to call him to account for choosing such servants, and are you, lost and terrible man, entitled to judge him therefor?"

"Very well," answered Kohlhaas, "if the sovereign does not cast me out I will return again to the community which he protects. Procure for me, I repeat it, safe conduct to Dresden; then I will disperse the band of men that I have collected in the castle at Lützen and I will once again lay my complaint, which was rejected, before the courts of the land."

With an expression of vexation, Luther tossed in a heap the papers that were lying on his desk, and was silent. The attitude of defiance which this singular man had assumed toward the state irritated him, and reflecting upon the judgment which Kohlhaas had issued at Kohlhaasenbrück against the Squire, he asked what it was that he demanded of the tribunal at Dresden. Kohlhaas answered, "The punishment of the Squire according to the law; restoration of the horses to their former condition; and compensation for the damages which I, as well as my groom Herse, who fell at Mühlberg, have suffered from the outrage perpetrated upon us."

Luther cried, "Compensation for damages! Money by the thousands, from Jews and Christians, on notes and securities, you have borrowed to defray the expenses of your wild revenge! Shall you put that amount also on the bill when it comes to reckoning up the costs?"

"God forbid!" answered Kohlhaas. "House and farm and the means that I possessed I do not demand back, any more than the expenses of my wife's funeral! Herse's old mother will present the bill for her son's medical treatment, as well as a list of those things which he lost at Tronka Castle; and the loss which I suffered on account of not selling the black horses the government may have estimated by an expert."

Luther exclaimed, as he gazed at him, "Mad, incomprehensible, and amazing man! After your sword has taken the most ferocious revenge upon the Squire which could well be imagined, what impels you to insist upon a judgment against him, the severity of which, when it is finally pronounced, will fall so lightly upon him?"

Kohlhaas answered, while a tear rolled down his cheek, "Most reverend Sir! It has cost me my wife; Kohlhaas intends to prove to the world that she did not perish in an unjust quarrel. Do you, in these particulars, yield to my will and let the court of justice speak; in all other points that may be contested I will yield to you."

Luther said, "See here, what you demand is just, if indeed the circumstances are such as is commonly reported; and if you had only succeeded in having your suit decided by the sovereign before you arbitrarily proceeded to avenge yourself, I do not doubt that your demands would have been granted, point for point. But, all things considered, would it not have been better for you to pardon the Squire for your Redeemer's sake, take back the black horses, thin and worn-out as they were, and mount and ride home to Kohlhaasenbrück to fatten them in your own stable!"

Kohlhaas answered, "Perhaps!" Then, stepping to the window, "Perhaps not, either! Had I known that I should be obliged to set them on their feet again with blood from the heart of my dear wife, I might, reverend Sir, perhaps have done as you say and not have considered a bushel of oats! But since they have now cost me so dear, let the matter run its course, say I; have judgment be pronounced as is due me, and have the Squire fatten my horses for me."

Turning back to his papers with conflicting thoughts, Luther said that he would enter into negotiations with the Elector on his behalf; in the mean time let him remain quietly in the castle at Lützen. If the sovereign would consent to accord him free-conduct, they would make the fact known to him by posting it publicly. "To be sure," he continued, as Kohlhaas bent to kiss his hand, "whether the Elector will be lenient, I do not know, for I have heard that he has collected an army and is about to start out to apprehend you in the castle at Lützen; however, as I have already told you, there shall be no lack of effort on my part" and, as he spoke, he got up from his chair prepared to dismiss him. Kohlhaas declared that Luther's intercession completely reassured him on that point, whereupon Luther bowed to him with a sweep of his hand. Kohlhaas, however, suddenly sank down on one knee before him and said he had still another favor to ask of him—the fact was, that at Whitsuntide, when it was his custom to receive the Holy Communion, he had failed to go to church on account of this warlike expedition of his. Would Luther have the goodness to receive his confession without further preparation and, in exchange, administer to him the blessed Holy Sacrament? Luther, after reflecting a short time, scanned his face, and said, "Yes, Kohlhaas, I will do so. But the Lord, whose body you desire, forgave his enemy. Will you likewise," he added, as the other looked at him disconcerted, "forgive the Squire who has offended you? Will you go to Tronka Castle, mount your black horses, ride them back to Kohlhaasenbrück and fatten them there?"

"Your Reverence!" said Kohlhaas flushing, and seized his hand "Well?"

"Even the Lord did not forgive all his enemies. Let me forgive the Elector, my two gentlemen the castellan and the steward, the lords Hinz and Kunz, and whoever else may have injured me in this affair; but, if it is possible, suffer me to force the Squire to fatten my black horses again for me."

At these words Luther turned his back on him, with a displeased glance, and rang the bell. In answer to the summons an amanuensis came into the anteroom with a light, and Kohlhaas, wiping his eyes, rose from his knees disconcerted; and since the amanuensis was working in vain at the door, which was bolted, and Luther had sat down again to his papers, Kohlhaas opened the door for the man. Luther glanced for an instant over his shoulder at the stranger, and said to the amanuensis, "Light the way!" whereupon the latter, somewhat surprised at the sight of the visitor, took down from the wall the key to the outside door and stepped back to the half-opened door of the room, waiting for the stranger to take his departure. Kohlhaas, holding his hat nervously in both hands, said, "And so, most reverend Sir, I cannot partake of the benefit of reconciliation, which I solicited of you?"

Luther answered shortly, "Reconciliation with your Savior—no! With the sovereign that depends upon the success of the attempt which I promised you to make." And then he motioned to the amanuensis to carry out, without further delay, the command he had given him. Kohlhaas laid both hands on his heart with an expression of painful emotion, and disappeared after the man who was lighting him down the stairs.

On the next morning Luther dispatched a message to the Elector of Saxony in which, after a bitter allusion to the lords, Hinz and Kunz Tronka, Chamberlain and Cup-bearer to his Highness, who, as was generally known, had suppressed the petition, he informed the sovereign, with the candor that was peculiar to him, that under such notorious circumstances there was nothing to do but to accept the proposition of the horse-dealer and to grant him an amnesty for what had occurred so that he might have opportunity to renew his lawsuit. Public opinion, Luther remarked, was on the side of this man to a very dangerous extent—so much so that, even in Wittenberg, which had three times been burnt down by him, there was a voice raised in his favor. And since, if his offer were refused, Kohlhaas would undoubtedly bring it to the knowledge of the people, accompanied by malicious comments, and the populace might easily be so far misled that nothing further could be done against him by the authorities of the state, Luther concluded that, in this extraordinary case, scruples about entering into negotiations with a subject who had taken up arms must be passed over; that, as a matter of fact, the latter, by the conduct which had been observed toward him, had in a sense been cast out of the body politic, and, in short, in order to put an end to the matter, he should be regarded rather as a foreign power which had attacked the land (and, since he was not a Saxon subject, he really might, in a way, be regarded as such), than as a rebel in revolt against the throne.

When the Elector received this letter there were present at the palace Prince Christiern of Meissen, Generalissimo of the Empire, uncle of that Prince Friedrich of Meissen who had been defeated at Mühlberg and was still laid up with his wounds, also the Grand Chancellor of the Tribunal, Count Wrede, Count Kallheim, President of the Chancery of State, and the two lords, Hinz and Kunz Tronka, the former Cup-bearer, the latter Chamberlain—all confidential friends of the sovereign from his youth. The Chamberlain, Sir Kunz, who in his capacity of privy councilor, attended to the private correspondence of his master and had the right to use his name and seal, was the first to speak. He once more explained in detail that never, on his own authority, would he have suppressed the complaint which the horse-dealer had lodged in court against his cousin the Squire, had it not been for the fact that, misled by false statements, he had believed it an absolutely unfounded and worthless piece of mischief-making. After this he passed on to consider the present state of affairs. He remarked that by neither divine nor human laws had the horse-dealer been warranted in wreaking such horrible vengeance as he had allowed himself to take for this mistake. The Chamberlain then proceeded to describe the glory that would fall upon the damnable head of the latter if they should negotiate with him as with a recognized military power, and the ignominy which would thereby be reflected upon the sacred person of the Elector seemed to him so intolerable that, carried away by the fire of his eloquence, he declared he would rather let worst come to worst, see the judgment of the mad rebel carried out and his cousin, the Squire, led off to Kohlhaasenbrück to fatten the black horses, than know that the proposition made by Dr. Luther had been accepted.

The Lord High Chancellor of the Tribunal of Justice, Count Wrede, turning half way round toward him, expressed regret that the Chamberlain had not, in the first instance, been inspired with such tender solicitude for the reputation of the sovereign as he was displaying in the solution of this undoubtedly delicate affair. He represented to the Elector his hesitation about employing the power of the state to carry out a manifestly unjust measure. He remarked, with a significant allusion to the great numbers which the horse-dealer was continually recruiting in the country, that the thread of the crime threatened in this way to be spun out indefinitely, and declared that the only way to sunder it and extricate the government happily from that ugly quarrel was to act with plain honesty and to make good, directly and without respect of person, the mistake which they had been guilty of committing.

Prince Christiern of Meissen, when asked by the Elector to express his opinion, turned deferentially toward the Grand Chancellor and declared that the latter's way of thinking naturally inspired in him the greatest respect, but, in wishing to aid Kohlhaas to secure justice, the Chancellor failed to consider that he was wronging Wittenberg, Leipzig, and the entire country that had been injured by him, in depriving them of their just claim for indemnity or at least for punishment of the culprit. The order of the state was so disturbed in its relation to this man that it would be difficult to set it right by an axiom taken from the science of law. Therefore, in accord with the opinion of the Chamberlain, he was in favor of employing the means appointed for such cases—that is to say, there should be gathered a force large enough to enable them either to capture or to crush the horse-dealer, who had planted himself in the castle at Lützen. The

Chamberlain brought over two chairs from the wall and obligingly placed them together in the middle of the room for the Elector and the Prince, saying, as he did so, that he was delighted to find that a man of the latter's uprightness and acumen agreed with him about the means to be employed in settling an affair of such varied aspect. The Prince, placing his hand on the chair without sitting down, looked at him, and assured him that he had little cause to rejoice on that account since the first step connected with this course would be the issuing of a warrant for his arrest, to be followed by a suit for misuse of the sovereign's name. For if necessity required that the veil be drawn before the throne of justice over a series of crimes, which finally would be unable to find room before the bar of judgment, since each led to another, and no end—this at least did not apply to the original offense which had given birth to them. First and foremost, he, the Chamberlain, must be tried for his life if the state was to be authorized to crush the horse-dealer, whose case, as was well known, was exceedingly just, and in whose hand they had placed the sword that he was wielding. The discomfited Chamberlain at these words gazed at the Elector, who turned away, his whole face flushing, and walked over to the window. After an embarrassing silence on all sides, Count Kallheim said that this was not the way to extricate themselves from the magic circle in which they were captive. His nephew, Prince Friedrich, might be put upon trial with equal justice, for in the peculiar expedition which he had undertaken against Kohlhaas he had overstepped his instructions in many ways—so much so that, if one were to inquire about the whole long list of those who had caused the embarrassment in which they now found themselves, he too would have to be named among them and called to account by the sovereign for what had occurred at Mühlberg.

While the Elector, with doubtful glances, walked up to his table, the Cup-bearer, Sir Hinz Tronka, began to speak in his turn. He did not understand, he said, how the governmental decree which was to be passed could escape men of such wisdom as were here assembled. The horse-dealer, so far as he knew, in return for mere safe-conduct to Dresden and a renewed investigation of his case, had promised to disband the force with which he had attacked the land. It did not follow from this, however, that he must be granted an amnesty for the wanton revenge he had taken into his own hands. These were two different legal concepts which Dr. Luther, as well as the council of state, seemed to have confounded. "When," he continued, laying his finger beside his nose, "the judgment concerning the black horses has been pronounced by the Tribunal at Dresden, no matter what it may be, nothing prevents us from imprisoning Kohlhaas on the ground of his incendiarism and robberies. That would be a diplomatic solution of the affair, which would unite the advantages of the opinion of both statesmen and would be sure to win the applause of the world and of posterity." The Prince, as well as the Lord Chancellor, answered this speech of Sir Hinz with a mere glance, and, as the discussion accordingly seemed at an end, the Elector said that he would turn over in his own mind, until the next sitting of the State Council, the various opinions which had been expressed before him. It seemed as if the preliminary measure mentioned by the Prince had deprived the Elector's heart, which was very sensitive where friendship was concerned, of the desire to proceed with the campaign against Kohlhaas, all the preparations for which were completed; at least he bade the Lord Chancellor, Count Wrede, whose opinion appeared to him the most expedient, to remain after the others left. The latter showed him letters from which it appeared that, as a matter of fact, the horse-dealer's forces had already come to number four hundred men; indeed, in view of the general discontent which prevailed all over the country on account of the misdemeanors of the Chamberlain, he might reckon on doubling or even tripling this number in a short time. Without further hesitation the Elector decided to accept the advice given him by Dr. Luther; accordingly he handed over to Count Wrede the entire management of the Kohlhaas affair. Only a few days later a placard appeared, the essence of which we give as follows:

"We, etc., etc., Elector of Saxony, in especially gracious consideration of the intercession made to us by Doctor Martin Luther, do grant to Michael Kohlhaas, horse-dealer from the territory of Brandenburg, safe-conduct to Dresden for the purpose of a renewed investigation of his case, on condition that, within three days after sight, he lay down the arms to which he has had recourse. It is to be understood, however, that in the unlikely event of Kohlhaas' suit concerning the black horses being rejected by the Tribunal at Dresden, he shall be prosecuted with all the severity of the law for arbitrarily undertaking to procure justice for himself. Should his suit, however, terminate otherwise, we will show mercy to him and his whole band, instead of inflicting deserved punishment, and a complete amnesty shall be accorded him for the acts of violence which he has committed in Saxony."

Kohlhaas had no sooner received through Dr. Luther a copy of this placard, which had been posted in all the public squares throughout the land, than, in spite of the conditional language in which it was couched, he immediately dispersed his whole band of followers with presents, expressions of gratitude, and appropriate admonitions. He deposited whatever he had taken in the way of money, weapons, and chattels, with the courts at Lützen, to be held as the property of the Elector, and after he had dispatched Waldmann to the bailiff at Kohlhaasenbrück with letters about repurchasing his farm, if that were still possible, and had sent Sternbald to Schwerin for his children whom he wished to have with him again, he left the castle at Lützen and went, without being recognized, to Dresden, carrying with him in bonds the remnant of his little property.

Day was just breaking and the whole city was still asleep when he knocked at the door of the little dwelling situated in the suburb of Pirna, which still, thanks to the honesty of the bailiff, belonged to him. Thomas, the old porter, in charge of the establishment, who on opening the door was surprised and startled to see his master, was told to take word to the Prince of Meissen, in the Government Office, that Kohlhaas the horse-dealer had arrived. The Prince of Meissen, on hearing this news, deemed it expedient to inform himself immediately of the relation in which they stood to this man. When, shortly afterward, he appeared with a retinue of knights and servants, he found an immense crowd of people already gathered in the streets leading to Kohlhaas' dwelling. The news that the destroying angel was there, who punished the oppressors of the people with fire and sword, had aroused all Dresden, the city as well as the suburbs. They were obliged to bolt the door of the house against the press of curious people, and the boys climbed up to the windows in order to get a peep at the incendiary, who was eating his breakfast inside.

As soon as the Prince, with the help of the guard who cleared the way for him, had pushed into the house and entered Kohlhaas' room, he asked the latter, who was standing half undressed before a table, whether he was Kohlhaas, the horse-dealer. Kohlhaas, drawing from his belt a wallet containing several papers concerning his affairs and handing it respectfully to the Prince, answered, "Yes;" and added that, in conformity with the immunity granted him by the sovereign, he had come to Dresden, after disbanding his force, in order to institute proceedings against Squire Wenzel Tronka on account of the black horses.

The Prince, after a hasty glance which took Kohlhaas in from head to foot, looked through the papers in the wallet and had him explain the nature of a certificate which he found there executed by the court at Lützen, concerning the deposit made in favor of the treasury of the Electorate. After he had further tested him with various questions about his children, his wealth, and the sort of life he intended to lead in the future, in order to find out what kind of man he was, and had concluded that in every respect they might set their minds at rest about him, he gave him back the documents and said that nothing now stood in the way of his lawsuit, and that, in order to institute it, he should just apply directly to the Lord High Chancellor of the Tribunal, Count Wrede himself. "In the meantime," said the Prince after a pause, crossing over to the window and gazing in amazement at the people gathered in front of the house, "you will be obliged to consent to a guard for the first few days, to protect you in your house as well as when you go out!" Kohlhaas looked down disconcerted, and was silent. "Well, no matter," said the Prince, leaving the window; "whatever happens, you have yourself to blame for it;" and with that he turned again toward the door with the intention of leaving the house. Kohlhaas, who had reflected, said "My lord, do as you like! If you will give me your word that the guard will be withdrawn as soon as I wish it, I have no objection to this measure." The Prince answered, "That is understood, of course." He informed the three foot-soldiers, who were appointed for this purpose, that the man in whose house they were to remain was free, and that it was merely for his protection that they were to follow him when he went out; he then saluted the horse-dealer with a condescending wave of the hand, and took his leave.

Toward midday Kohlhaas went to Count Wrede, Lord High Chancellor of the Tribunal; he was escorted by his three foot-soldiers and followed by an innumerable crowd, who, having been warned by the police, did not try to harm him in any way. The Chancellor received him in his antechamber with benignity and kindness, conversed with him for two whole hours, and after he had had the entire course of the affair related to him from beginning to end, referred Kohlhaas to a celebrated lawyer in the city who was a member of the Tribunal, so that he might have the complaint drawn up and presented immediately.

Kohlhaas, without further delay, betook himself to the lawyer's house and had the suit drawn up exactly like the original one which had been quashed. He demanded the punishment of the Squire according to law, the restoration of the horses to their former condition, and compensation for the damages he had sustained as well as for those suffered by his groom, Herse, who had fallen at Mühlberg—in behalf of the latter's old mother. When this was done Kohlhaas returned home, accompanied by the crowd that still continued to gape at him, firmly resolved in his mind not to leave the house again unless called away by important business.

In the mean time the Squire had been released from his imprisonment in Wittenberg, and after recovering from a dangerous attack of erysipelas which had caused inflammation of his foot, had been summoned by the Supreme Court in peremptory terms to present himself in Dresden to answer the suit instituted against him by the horse-dealer, Kohlhaas, with regard to a pair of black horses which had been unlawfully taken from him and worked to death. The Tronka brothers, the Chamberlain and the Cupbearer, cousins of the Squire, at whose house he alighted, received him with the greatest bitterness and contempt. They called him a miserable good-for-nothing, who had brought shame and disgrace on the whole family, told him that he would inevitably lose his suit, and called upon him to prepare at once to produce the black horses, which he would be condemned to fatten to the scornful laughter of the world. The Squire answered in a weak and trembling voice that he was more deserving of pity than any other man on earth. He swore that he had known but little about the whole cursed affair which had plunged him into misfortune, and that the castellan and the steward were to blame for everything, because they, without his knowledge or consent, had used the horses in getting in the crops and, by overworking them, partly in their own fields, had rendered them unfit for further use. He sat down as he said this and begged them not to mortify and insult him and thus wantonly cause a relapse of the illness from which he had but recently recovered.

Since there was nothing else to be done, the next day, at the request of their cousin, the Squire, the lords Hinz and Kunz, who possessed estates in the neighborhood of Tronka Castle, which had been burned down, wrote to their stewards and to the farmers living there for information about the black horses which had been lost on that unfortunate day and not heard of since. But on account of the complete destruction of the castle and the massacre of most of the inhabitants, all that they could learn was that a servant, driven by blows dealt with the flat of the incendiary's sword, had rescued them from the burning shed in which they were standing, but that afterward, to the question where he should take them and what he should do with them, he had been answered by a kick from the savage madman. The Squire's gouty old housekeeper, who had fled to Meissen, assured the latter, in reply to his written inquiry, that on the morning after that horrible night the servant had gone off with the horses toward the Brandenburg border, but all inquiries which were made there proved vain, and some error seemed to lie at the bottom of this information, as the Squire had no servant whose home was in Brandenburg or even on the road thither. Some men from Dresden, who had been in Wilsdruf a few days after the burning of Tronka Castle, declared that, at the time named, a groom had arrived in that place, leading two horses by the halter, and, as the animals were very sick and could go no further, he had left them in the cow-stable of a shepherd who had offered to restore them to good condition. For a variety of reasons it seemed very probable that these were the black horses for which search was being made, but persons coming from Wilsdruf declared that the shepherd had already traded them off again, no one knew to whom; and a third rumor, the originator of which could not be discovered, even asserted that the two horses had in the mean time passed peacefully away and been buried in the carrion pit at Wilsdruf.

This turn of affairs, as can be easily understood, was the most pleasing to the lords Hinz and Kunz, as they were thus relieved of the necessity of fattening the blacks in their stables, the Squire, their cousin, no longer having any stables of his own. They wished, however, for the sake of absolute security, to verify this circumstance. Sir Wenzel Tronka, therefore, in his capacity as hereditary feudal lord with the right of judicature, addressed a letter to the magistrates at Wilsdruf, in which, after a minute description of the black horses, which, as he said, had been intrusted to his care and lost through an accident, he begged them to be so obliging as to ascertain their present whereabouts, and to urge and admonish the owner, whoever he might be, to deliver them at the stables of the Chamberlain, Sir Kunz, in Dresden, and be generously reimbursed for all costs. Accordingly, a few days later, the man to whom the shepherd in Wilsdruf had sold them did actually appear with the horses, thin and staggering, tied to the tailboard of his cart, and led them to the marketplace in Dresden. As the bad luck of Sir Wenzel and still more of honest Kohlhaas would have it, however, the man happened to be the knacker from Döbeln.

As soon as Sir Wenzel, in the presence of the Chamberlain, his cousin, learned from an indefinite rumor that a man had arrived in the city with two black horses which had escaped from the burning of Tronka Castle, both gentlemen, accompanied by a few servants hurriedly collected in the house, went to the palace square where the man had stopped, intending, if the two animals proved to be those belonging to Kohlhaas, to make good the expenses the man had incurred and take the horses home with them. But how disconcerted were the knights to see a momentarily increasing crowd of people, who had been attracted by the spectacle, already standing around the two-wheeled cart to which the horses were fastened! Amid uninterrupted laughter they were calling to one another that the horses, on account of which the whole state was tottering, already belonged to the knacker! The Squire who had gone around the cart and gazed at the miserable animals, which seemed every moment about to expire, said in an embarrassed way that those were not the horses which he had taken from Kohlhaas; but Sir Kunz, the Chamberlain, casting at him a look of speechless rage which, had it been of iron, would have dashed him to pieces, and throwing back his cloak to disclose his orders and chain, stepped up to the knacker and asked if those were the black horses which the shepherd at Wilsdruf had gained possession of, and for which Squire Wenzel Tronka, to whom they belonged, had made requisition through the magistrate of that place.

The knacker who, with a pail of water in his hand, was busy watering a fat, sturdy horse that was drawing his cart asked—"The blacks?" Then he put down the pail, took the bit out of the horse's mouth, and explained that the black horses which were tied to the tailboard of the cart had been sold to him by the swineherd in Hainichen; where the latter had obtained them and whether they came from the shepherd at Wilsdruf—that he did not know. "He had been told," he continued, taking up the pail again and propping it between the pole of the cart and his knee—"he had been told by the messenger of the court at Wilsdruf to take the horses to the house of the Tronkas in Dresden, but the Squire to whom he had been directed was named Kunz." With these words he turned around with the rest of the water which the horse had left in the pail, and emptied it out on the pavement. The Chamberlain, who was beset by the stares of the laughing, jeering crowd and could not induce the fellow, who was attending to his business with phlegmatic zeal, to look at him, said that he was the Chamberlain Kunz Tronka. The black horses, however, which he was to get possession of, had to be those belonging to the Squire, his cousin; they must have been given to the shepherd at Wilsdruf by a stable-man who had run away from Tronka Castle at the time of the fire; moreover, they must be the two horses that originally had belonged to the horse-dealer Kohlhaas. He asked the fellow, who was standing there with his legs apart, pulling up his trousers, whether he did not know something about all this. Had not the swineherd of Hainichen, he went on, perhaps purchased these horses from the shepherd at Wilsdruf, or from a third person, who in turn had bought them from the latter?—for everything depended on this circumstance.

The knacker replied that he had been ordered to go with the black horses to Dresden and was to receive the money for them in the house of the Tronkas. He did not understand what the Squire was talking about, and whether it was Peter or Paul, or the shepherd in Wilsdruf, who had owned them before the swineherd in Hainichen, was all one to him so long as they had not been stolen; and with this he went off, with his whip across his broad back, to a public house which stood in the square, with the intention of getting some breakfast, as he was very hungry.

The Chamberlain, who for the life of him didn't know what he should do with the horses which the swineherd of Hainichen had sold to the knacker of Döbeln, unless they were those on which the devil was riding through Saxony, asked the Squire to say something; but when the latter with white, trembling lips replied that it would be advisable to buy the black horses whether they belonged to Kohlhaas or not, the Chamberlain, cursing the father and mother who had given birth to the Squire, stepped aside out of the crowd and threw back his cloak, absolutely at a loss to know what he should do or leave undone. Defiantly determined not to leave the square just because the rabble were staring at him derisively and with their handkerchiefs pressed tight over their mouths seemed to be waiting only for him to depart before bursting out into laughter, he called to Baron Wenk, an acquaintance who happened to be riding by, and begged him to stop at the house of the Lord High Chancellor, Count Wrede, and through the latter's instrumentality to have Kohlhaas brought there to look at the black horses.

When the Baron, intent upon this errand, entered the chamber of the Lord High Chancellor, it so happened that Kohlhaas was just then present, having been summoned by a messenger of the court to give certain explanations of which they stood in need concerning the deposit in Lützen. While the Chancellor, with an annoyed look, rose from his chair and asked the horse-dealer, whose person was unknown to the Baron, to step to one side with his papers, the latter informed him of the dilemma in which the lords Tronka found themselves. He explained that the knacker from Döbeln, acting on a defective requisition from the court at Wilsdruf, had appeared with horses whose condition was so frightful that Squire Wenzel could not help hesitating to pronounce them the ones belonging to Kohlhaas. In case they were to be taken from the knacker notwithstanding, and an attempt made to restore them to good condition in the stables of the knights, an ocular inspection by Kohlhaas would first be necessary in order to establish the aforesaid circumstance beyond doubt. "Will you therefore have the goodness," he concluded, "to have a guard fetch the horse-dealer from his house and conduct him to the market-place where the horses are standing!" The Lord High Chancellor, taking his glasses from his nose, said that the Baron was laboring under a double delusion first, in thinking that the fact in question could be ascertained only by means of an ocular inspection by Kohlhaas, and then, in imagining that he, the Chancellor, possessed the authority to have Kohlhaas taken by a guard wherever the Squire happened to wish. With this he presented to him Kohlhaas who was standing behind him, and sitting down and putting on his glasses again, begged him to apply to the horse-dealer himself in the matter.

Kohlhaas, whose expression gave no hint of what was going on in his mind, said that he was ready to follow the Baron to the market-place and inspect the black horses which the knacker had brought to the city. As the disconcerted Baron faced around toward him, Kohlhaas stepped up to the table of the Chancellor, and, after taking time to explain to him, with the help of the papers in his wallet, several matters concerning the deposit in Lützen, took his leave. The Baron, who had walked over to the window, his face suffused with a deep blush, likewise made his adieux, and both, escorted by the three foot-soldiers assigned by the Prince of Meissen, took their way to the Palace square attended by a great crowd of people.

In the mean time the Chamberlain, Sir Kunz, in spite of the protests of several friends who had joined him, had stood his ground among the people, opposite the knacker of Döbeln. As soon as the

Baron and the horse-dealer appeared he went up to the latter and, holding his sword proudly and ostentatiously under his arm, asked if the horses standing behind the wagon were his.

The horse-dealer, turning modestly toward the gentleman who had asked him the question and who was unknown to him, touched his hat; then, without answering, he walked toward the knacker's cart, surrounded by all the knights. The animals were standing there on unsteady legs, with heads bowed down to the ground, making no attempt to eat the hay which the knacker had placed before them. Kohlhaas stopped a dozen feet away, and after a hasty glance turned back again to the Chamberlain, saying, "My lord, the knacker is quite right; the horses which are fastened to his cart belong to me!" As he spoke he looked around at the whole circle of knights, touched his hat once more, and left the square, accompanied by his guard.

At these words the Chamberlain, with a hasty step that made the plume of his helmet tremble, strode up to the knacker and threw him a purse full of money. And while the latter, holding the purse in his hand, combed the hair back from his forehead with a leaden comb and stared at the money, Sir Kunz ordered a groom to untie the horses and lead them home. The groom, at the summons of his master, left a group of his friends and relatives among the crowd; his face flushed slightly, but he did, nevertheless, go up to the horses, stepping over a big puddle that had formed at their feet. No sooner, however, had he taken hold of the halter to untie them, than Master Himboldt, his cousin, seized him by the arm, and with the words, "You shan't touch the knacker's jades!" hurled him away from the cart. Then, stepping back unsteadily over the puddle, the Master turned toward the Chamberlain, who was standing there, speechless with astonishment at this incident, and added that he must get a knacker's man to do him such a service as that. The Chamberlain, foaming with rage, stared at Master Himboldt for a moment, then turned about and, over the heads of the knights who surrounded him, called for the guard. When, in obedience to the orders of Baron Wenk, an officer with some of the Elector's bodyguards had arrived from the palace, Sir Kunz gave him a short account of the shameful way in which the burghers of the city permitted themselves to instigate revolt, and called upon the officer to place the ringleader, Master Himboldt, under arrest. Seizing the Master by the chest, the Chamberlain accused him of having maltreated and thrust away from the cart the groom who, at his orders, was unhitching the black horses. The Master, freeing himself from the Chamberlain's grasp with a skilful twist which forced the latter to step back, cried, "My lord, showing a boy of twenty what he ought to do is not instigating him to revolt! Ask him whether, contrary to all that is customary and decent, he cares to have anything to do with those horses that are tied to the cart. If he wants to do it after what I have said, well and good. For all I care, he may flay and skin them now."

At these words the Chamberlain turned round to the groom and asked him if he had any scruples about fulfilling his command to untie the horses which belonged to Kohlhaas and lead them home. When the groom, stepping back among the citizens, answered timidly that the horses must be made honorable once more before that could be expected of him, the Chamberlain followed him, tore from the young man's head the hat which was decorated with the badge of his house, and, after trampling it under his feet, drew his sword and with furious blows drove the groom instantly from the square and from his service. Master Himboldt cried, "Down with the bloodthirsty madman, friends!" And while the citizens, outraged at this scene, crowded together and forced back the guard, he came up behind the Chamberlain and threw him down, tore off his cloak, collar, and helmet, wrenched the sword from his hand, and dashed it with a furious fling far away across the square.

In vain did the Squire Wenzel, as he worked his way out of the crowd, call to the knights to go to his cousin's aid; even before they had started to rescue him, they had been so scattered by the rush of the mob that the Chamberlain, who in falling had injured his head, was exposed to the full wrath of the crowd. The only thing that saved him was the appearance of a troop of mounted soldiers who chanced to be crossing the square, and whom the officer of the Elector's body-guards called to his assistance. The officer, after dispersing the crowd, seized the furious Master Himboldt, and, while some of the troopers bore him off to prison, two friends picked up the unfortunate Chamberlain, who was covered with blood, and carried him home.

Such was the unfortunate outcome of the well-meant and honest attempt to procure the horse-dealer satisfaction for the injustice that had been committed against him. The knacker of Döbeln, whose business was concluded, and who did not wish to delay any longer, tied the horses to a lamppost, since the crowd was beginning to scatter, and there they remained the whole day through without any one's bothering about them, an object of mockery for the street-arabs and loafers. Finally, since they lacked any sort of care and attention, the police were obliged to take them in hand, and, toward evening, the knacker of Dresden was called to carry them off to the knacker's house outside the city to await further instructions.

This incident, as little as the horse-dealer was in reality to blame for it, nevertheless awakened throughout the country, even among the more moderate and better class of people, a sentiment extremely dangerous to the success of his lawsuit. The relation of this man to the state was felt to be quite intolerable and, in private houses as well as in public places, the opinion gained ground that it would be better to commit an open injustice against him and quash the whole lawsuit anew, rather than, for the mere sake of satisfying his mad obstinacy, to accord him in so trivial a matter justice which he had wrung from them by deeds of violence.

To complete the ruin of poor Kohlhaas, it was the Lord High Chancellor himself, animated by too great probity, and a consequent hatred of the Tronka family, who helped strengthen and spread this sentiment. It was highly improbable that the horses, which were now being cared for by the knacker of Dresden, would ever be restored to the condition they were in when they left the stables at Kohlhaasenbrück. However, granted that this might be possible by skilful and constant care, nevertheless the disgrace which, as a result of the existing circumstances, had fallen upon the Squire's family was so great that, in consideration of the political importance which the house possessed being, as it was, one of the oldest and noblest families in the land—nothing seemed more just and expedient than to arrange a money indemnity for the horses. In spite of this, a few days later, when the President, Count Kallheim, in the name of the Chamberlain, who was deterred by his sickness, sent a letter to the Chancellor containing this proposition, the latter did indeed send a communication to Kohlhaas in which he admonished him not to decline such a proposition should it be made to him; but in a short and rather curt answer to the President himself the Chancellor begged him not to bother him with private commissions in this matter and advised the Chamberlain to apply to the horse-dealer himself, whom he described as a very just and modest man. The horse-dealer, whose will was, in fact, broken by the incident which had occurred in the market-place, was, in conformity with the advice of the Lord Chancellor, only waiting for an overture on the part of the Squire or his relatives in order to meet them half-way with perfect willingness and forgiveness for all that had happened; but to make this overture entailed too great a sacrifice of dignity on the part of the proud knights. Very much incensed by the answer they had received from the Lord Chancellor, they showed the same to the Elector, who on the morning of the following day had visited the Chamberlain in his room where he was confined to his bed with his wounds.

In a voice rendered weak and pathetic by his condition, the Chamberlain asked the Elector whether, after risking his life to settle this affair according to his sovereign's wishes, he must also expose his honor to the censure of the world and to appear with a request for relenting and compromise before a man who had brought every imaginable shame and disgrace on him and his family.

The Elector, after having read the letter, asked Count Kallheim in an embarrassed way whether, without further communication with Kohlhaas, the Tribunal were not authorized to base its decision on the fact that the horses could not be restored to their original condition, and in conformity therewith to draw up the judgment just as if the horses were dead, on the sole basis of a money indemnity.

The Count answered, "Most gracious sovereign, they are dead; they are dead in the sight of the law because they have no value, and they will be so physically before they can be brought from the knacker's house to the knights' stables." To this the Elector, putting the letter in his pocket, replied that he would himself speak to the Lord Chancellor about it. He spoke soothingly to the Chamberlain, who raised himself on his elbow and seized his hand in gratitude, and, after lingering a moment to urge him to take care of his health, rose with a very gracious air and left the room.

Thus stood affairs in Dresden, when from the direction of Lützen there gathered over poor Kohlhaas another thunder-storm, even more serious, whose lightning-flash the crafty knights were clever enough to draw down upon the horse-dealer's unlucky head. It so happened that one of the band of men that Kohlhaas had collected and turned off again after the appearance of the electoral amnesty, Johannes Nagelschmidt by name, had found it expedient, some weeks later, to muster again on the Bohemian frontier a part of this rabble which was ready to take part in any infamy, and to continue on his own account the profession on the track of which Kohlhaas had put him. This good-for-nothing fellow called himself a vicegerent of Kohlhaas, partly to inspire with fear the officers of the law who were after him, and partly, by the use of familiar methods, to beguile the country people into participating in his rascalities. With a cleverness which he had learned from his master, he had it noised abroad that the amnesty had not been kept in the case of several men who had quietly returned to their homes—indeed that Kohlhaas himself had, with a faithlessness which cried aloud to heaven, been arrested on his arrival in Dresden and placed under a guard. He carried it so far that, in manifestos which were very similar to those of Kohlhaas, his incendiary band appeared as an army raised solely for the glory of God and meant to watch over the observance of the amnesty promised by the Elector. All this, as we have already said, was done by no means for the glory of God nor out of attachment for Kohlhaas, whose fate was a matter of absolute indifference to the outlaws, but in order to enable them, under cover of such dissimulation, to burn and plunder with the greater ease and impunity.

When the first news of this reached Dresden the knights could not conceal their joy over the occurrence, which lent an entirely different aspect to the whole matter. With wise and displeased allusions they recalled the mistake which had been made when, in spite of their urgent and repeated warnings, an amnesty had been granted Kohlhaas, as if those who had been in favor of it had had the deliberate intention of giving to miscreants of all kinds the signal to follow in his footsteps. Not content with crediting Nagelschmidt's pretext that he had taken up arms merely to lend support and security to his oppressed master, they even expressed the decided opinion that his whole course was nothing but an enterprise contrived by Kohlhaas in order to frighten the government, and to hasten and insure the rendering of a verdict, which, point for point, should satisfy his mad obstinacy. Indeed the Cup-bearer, Sir Hinz, went so far as to declare to some hunting-pages and courtiers who had gathered round him after dinner in the Elector's antechamber that the breaking up of the marauding band in Lützen had been but a cursed pretense. He was very merry over the Lord High Chancellor's alleged love of justice; by cleverly connecting various circumstances he proved that the band was still extant in the forests of the Electorate and was only waiting for a signal from the horse-dealer to break out anew with fire and sword.

Prince Christiern of Meissen, very much displeased at this turn in affairs, which threatened to fleck his sovereign's honor in the most painful manner, went immediately to the palace to confer with the

Elector. He saw quite clearly that it would be to the interest of the knights to ruin Kohlhaas, if possible, on the ground of new crimes, and he begged the Elector to give him permission to have an immediate judicial examination of the horse-dealer. Kohlhaas, somewhat astonished at being conducted to the Government Office by a constable, appeared with his two little boys, Henry and Leopold, in his arms; for Sternbald, his servant, had arrived the day before with his five children from Mecklenburg, where they had been staying. When Kohlhaas had started to leave for the Government Office the two boys had burst into childish tears, begging him to take them along, and various considerations too intricate to unravel made him decide to pick them up and carry them with him to the hearing. Kohlhaas placed the children beside him, and the Prince, after looking benevolently at them and asking, with friendly interest, their names and ages, went on to inform Kohlhaas what liberties Nagelschmidt, his former follower, was taking in the valleys of the Ore Mountains, and handing him the latter's so-called mandates he told him to produce whatever he had to offer for his vindication. Although the horse-dealer was deeply alarmed by these shameful and traitorous papers, he nevertheless had little difficulty in explaining satisfactorily to so upright a man as the Prince the groundlessness of the accusations brought against him on this score. Besides the fact that, so far as he could observe, he did not, as the matter now stood, need any help as yet from a third person in bringing about the decision of his lawsuit, which was proceeding most favorably, some papers which he had with him and showed to the Prince made it appear highly improbable that Nagelschmidt should be inclined to render him help of that sort, for, shortly before the dispersion of the band in Lützen, he had been on the point of having the fellow hanged for a rape committed in the open country, and other rascalities. Only the appearance of the electoral amnesty had saved Nagelschmidt, as it had severed all relations between them, and on the next day they had parted as mortal enemies.

Kohlhaas, with the Prince's approval of the idea, sat down and wrote a letter to Nagelschmidt in which he declared that the latter's pretense of having taken the field in order to maintain the amnesty which had been violated with regard to him and his band, was a disgraceful and vicious fabrication. He told him that, on his arrival in Dresden, he had neither been imprisoned nor handed over to a guard, also that his lawsuit was progressing exactly as he wished, and, as a warning for the rabble who had gathered around Nagelschmidt, he gave him over to the full vengeance of the law for the outrages which he had committed in the Ore Mountains after the publication of the amnesty. Some portions of the criminal prosecution which the horse-dealer had instituted against him in the castle at Lützen on account of the above-mentioned disgraceful acts, were also appended to the letter to enlighten the people concerning the good-for-nothing fellow, who even at that time had been destined for the gallows, and, as already stated, had only been saved by the edict issued by the Elector. In consequence of this letter the Prince appeased Kohlhaas' displeasure at the suspicion which, of necessity, they had been obliged to express in this hearing; he went on to declare that, while he remained in Dresden, the amnesty granted him should not be violated in any way; then, after presenting to the boys some fruit that was on his table, he shook hands with them once more, saluted Kohlhaas, and dismissed him.

The Lord High Chancellor, who nevertheless recognized the danger that was threatening the horse-dealer, did his utmost to bring his lawsuit to an end before it should be complicated and confused by new developments; this, however, was exactly what the diplomatic knights desired and aimed at. Instead of silently acknowledging their guilt, as at first, and obtaining merely a less severe sentence, they now began with pettifogging and crafty subterfuges to deny this guilt itself entirely. Sometimes they pretended that the black horses belonging to Kohlhaas had been detained at Tronka Castle on the arbitrary authority of the castellan and the steward, and that the Squire had known little, if anything, of their actions. At other times they declared that, even on their arrival at the castle, the animals had been suffering from a violent and dangerous cough, and, in confirmation of the fact, they referred to witnesses whom they pledged themselves to produce. Forced to withdraw these arguments after many long-drawn-out investigations and explanations, they even cited an electoral edict of twelve years before, in which the importation of horses from Brandenburg into Saxony had actually been forbidden, on account of a plague among the cattle. This circumstance, according to them, made it as clear as day that the Squire not only had the authority, but also was under obligation, to hold up the horses that Kohlhaas had brought across the border. Kohlhaas, meanwhile, had bought back his farm at Kohlhaasenbrück from the honest bailiff, in return for a small compensation for the loss sustained. He wished, apparently in connection with the legal settlement of this business, to leave Dresden for some days and return to his home, in which determination, however, the above-mentioned matter of business, imperative as it may actually have been on account of sowing the winter crops, undoubtedly played less part than the intention of testing his position under such unusual and critical circumstances. He may perhaps also have been influenced by reasons of still another kind which we will leave to every one who is acquainted with his own heart to divine.

In pursuance of this resolve he betook himself to the Lord Chancellor, leaving behind the guard which had been assigned to him. He carried with him the letters from the bailiff, and explained that if, as seemed to be the case, he were not urgently needed in court, he would like to leave the city and go to Brandenburg for a week or ten days, within which time he promised to be back again. The Lord High Chancellor, looking down with a displeased and dubious expression, replied that he must acknowledge that Kohlhaas' presence was more necessary just then than ever, as the court, on account of the prevaricating and tricky tactics of the opposition, required his statements and explanations at a thousand points that could not be foreseen. However, when Kohlhaas referred him to his lawyer, who was well informed concerning the lawsuit, and with modest importunity persisted in his request, promising to confine his absence to a week, the Lord Chancellor, after a pause, said briefly, as he dismissed him, that he hoped that Kohlhaas would apply to Prince Christiern of Meissen for passports.

Kohlhaas, who could read the Lord Chancellor's face perfectly, was only strengthened in his determination. He sat down immediately and, without giving any reason, asked the Prince of Meissen, as head of the Government Office, to furnish him passports for a week's journey to Kohlhaasenbrück and back. In reply to this letter he received a cabinet order signed by the Governor of the Palace, Baron Siegfried Wenk, to the effect that his request for passports to Kohlhaasenbrück would be laid before his serene highness the Elector, and as soon as his gracious consent had been received the passports would be sent to him. When Kohlhaas inquired of his lawyer how the cabinet order came to be signed by a certain Baron, Siegfried Wenk, and not by Prince Christiern of Meissen to whom he had applied, he was told that the Prince had set out for his estates three days before, and during his absence the affairs of the Government

Office had been put in the hands of the Governor of the Palace, Baron Siegfried Wenk, a cousin of the gentleman of the same name who has been already mentioned.

Kohlhaas, whose heart was beginning to beat uneasily amid all these complications, waited several days for the decision concerning his petition which had been laid before the person of the sovereign with such a surprising amount of formality. A week passed, however, and more than a week, without the arrival of this decision; nor had judgment been pronounced by the Tribunal, although it had been definitely promised him. Finally, on the twelfth day, Kohlhaas, firmly resolved to force the government to proclaim its intentions toward him, let them be what they would, sat down and, in an urgent request, once more asked the Government Office for the desired passports. On the evening of the following day, which had likewise passed without the expected answer, he was walking up and down, thoughtfully considering his position and especially the amnesty procured for him by Dr. Luther, when, on approaching the window of his little back room, he was astonished not to see the soldiers in the little out-building on the courtyard which he had designated as quarters for the guard assigned him by the Prince of Meissen at the time of his arrival. He called Thomas, the old porter, to him and asked what it meant. The latter answered with a sigh, "Sir, something is wrong! The soldiers, of whom there are more today than usual, distributed themselves around the whole house when it began to grow dark; two with shield and spear are standing in the street before the front door, two are at the back door in the garden, and two others are lying on a truss of straw in the vestibule and say that they are going to sleep there."

Kohlhaas grew pale and turned away, adding that it really did not matter, provided they were still there, and that when Thomas went down into the corridor he should place a light so that the soldiers could see. Then he opened the shutter of the front window under the pretext of emptying a vessel, and convinced himself of the truth of the circumstance of which the old man had informed him, for just at that moment the guard was actually being changed without a sound, a precaution which had never before entered any one's head as long as the arrangement had existed. After which, Kohlhaas, having made up his mind immediately what he would do on the morrow, went to bed, though, to be sure, he felt little desire to sleep. For nothing in the course of the government with which he was dealing displeased him more than this outward form of justice, while in reality it was violating in his case the amnesty promised him, and in case he were to be considered really a prisoner as could no longer be doubted he intended to wring from the government the definite and straightforward statement that such was the case.

In accordance with this plan, at earliest dawn he had Sternbald, his groom, harness his wagon and drive up to the door, intending, as he explained, to drive to Lockwitz to see the steward, an old acquaintance of his, who had met him a few days before in Dresden and had invited him and his children to visit him some time. The soldiers, who, putting their heads together, had watched the stir which these preparations were causing in the household, secretly sent off one of their number to the city and, a few minutes later, a government clerk appeared at the head of several constables and went into the house opposite, pretending to have some business there. Kohlhaas, who was occupied in dressing his boys, likewise noticed the commotion and intentionally kept the wagon waiting in front of the house longer than was really necessary. As soon as he saw that the arrangements of the police were completed, without paying any attention to them he came out before the house with his children. He said, in passing, to the group of soldiers standing in the doorway that they did not need to follow him; then he lifted the boys into the wagon and kissed and comforted the weeping little girls who, in obedience to his orders, were to remain behind with the daughter of the old porter. He had no sooner climbed up on the wagon himself than the government clerk, with the constables who accompanied him, stepped up from the opposite house and asked where he was going. To the answer of Kohlhaas that he was going to Lockwitz to see his friend, the steward, who a few days before had invited him and his two boys to visit him in the country, the clerk replied that in that case Kohlhaas must wait a few moments, as some mounted soldiers would accompany him in obedience to the order of the Prince of Meissen. From his seat on the wagon Kohlhaas asked smilingly whether he thought that his life would not be safe in the house of a friend who had offered to entertain him at his table for a day.

The official answered in a pleasant, joking way that the danger was certainly not very great, adding that the soldiers were not to incommode him in any way. Kohlhaas replied, seriously, that on his arrival in Dresden the Prince of Meissen had left it to his own choice whether he would make use of the guard or not, and as the clerk seemed surprised at this circumstance and with carefully chosen phrases reminded him that he had employed the guard during the whole time of his presence in the city, the horse-dealer related to him the incident which had led to the placing of the soldiers in his house. The clerk assured him that the orders of the Governor of the Palace, Baron Wenk, who was at that moment head of the police force, made it his duty to watch over Kohlhaas' person continually, and begged him, if he would not consent to the escort, to go to the Government Office himself so as to correct the mistake which must exist in the matter. Kohlhaas threw a significant glance at the clerk and, determined to put an end to the matter by hook or by crook, said that he would do so. With a beating heart he got down from the wagon, had the porter carry the children back into the corridor, and while his servant remained before the house with the wagon, Kohlhaas went off to the Government Office, accompanied by the clerk and his guard.

It happened that the Governor of the Palace, Baron Wenk, was busy at the moment inspecting a band of Nagelschmidt's followers who had been captured in the neighborhood of Leipzig and brought to Dresden the previous evening. The knights who were with the Governor were just questioning the fellows about a great many things which the government was anxious to learn from them, when the horse-dealer entered the room with his escort. The Baron, as soon as he caught sight of Kohlhaas, went up to him and asked him what he wanted, while the knights grew suddenly silent and interrupted the interrogation of the prisoners. When Kohlhaas had respectfully submitted to him his purpose of going to dine with the steward at Lockwitz, and expressed the wish to be allowed to leave behind the soldiers of whom he had no need, the Baron, changing color and seeming to swallow some words of a different nature, answered that Kohlhaas would do well to stay quietly at home and to postpone for the present the feast at the Lockwitz steward's. With that he turned to the clerk, thus cutting short the whole conversation, and told him that the order which he had given him with regard to this man held good, and that the latter must not leave the city unless accompanied by six mounted soldiers.

Kohlhaas asked whether he were a prisoner, and whether he should consider that the amnesty which had been solemnly promised to him before the eyes of the whole world had been broken. At which the Baron, his face turning suddenly a fiery red, wheeled around and, stepping close up to him and looking him in the eyes, answered,

"Yes! Yes! Yes!" Then he turned his back upon him and, leaving Kohlhaas standing there, returned to Nagelschmidt's followers.

At this Kohlhaas left the room, and although he realized that the steps he had taken had rendered much more difficult the only means of rescue that remained, namely, flight, he nevertheless was glad he had done as he had, since he was now, on his part, likewise released from obligation to observe the conditions of the amnesty. When he reached home he had the horses unharnessed, and, very sad and shaken, went to his room accompanied by the government clerk. While this man, in a way which aroused the horse-dealer's disgust, assured him that it must all be due to a misunderstanding which would shortly be cleared up, the constables, at a sign from him, bolted all the exits which led from the house into the courtyard. At the same time the clerk assured Kohlhaas that the main entrance at the front of the house still remained open and that he could use it as he pleased.

Nagelschmidt, meanwhile, had been so hard pushed on all sides by constables and soldiers in the woods of the Ore Mountains, that, entirely deprived, as he was, of the necessary means of carrying through a role of the kind which he had undertaken, he hit upon the idea of inducing Kohlhaas to take sides with him in reality. As a traveler passing that way had informed him fairly accurately of the status of Kohlhaas' lawsuit in Dresden, he believed that, in spite of the open enmity which existed between them, he could persuade the horse-dealer to enter into a new alliance with him. He therefore sent off one of his men to him with a letter, written in almost unreadable German, to the effect that if he would come to Altenburg and resume command of the band which had gathered there from the remnants of his former troops who had been dispersed, he, Nagelschmidt, was ready to assist him to escape from his imprisonment in Dresden by furnishing him with horses, men, and money. At the same time he promised Kohlhaas that, in the future, he would be more obedient and in general better and more orderly than he had been before; and to prove his faithfulness and devotion he pledged himself to come in person to the outskirts of Dresden in order to effect Kohlhaas' deliverance from his prison.

The fellow charged with delivering this letter had the bad luck, in a village close to Dresden, to be seized with a violent fit, such as he had been subject to from childhood. In this situation, the letter which he was carrying in his vest was found by the persons who came to his assistance; the man himself, as soon as he had recovered, was arrested and transported to the Government Office under guard, accompanied by a large crowd of people. As soon as the Governor of the Palace, Wenk, had read this letter, he went immediately to the palace to see the Elector; here he found present also the President of the Chancery of State, Count Kallheim, and the lords Kunz and Hinz, the former of whom had recovered from his wounds. These gentlemen were of the opinion that Kohlhaas should be arrested without delay and brought to trial on the charge of secret complicity with Nagelschmidt. They went on to demonstrate that such a letter could not have been written unless there had been preceding letters written by the horse-dealer, too, and that it would inevitably result in a wicked and criminal union of their forces for the purpose of plotting fresh iniquities.

The Elector steadfastly refused to violate, merely on the ground of this letter, the safe-conduct he had solemnly promised to Kohlhaas. He was more inclined to believe that Nagelschmidt's letter made it rather probable that no previous connection had existed between them, and all he would do to clear up the matter was to assent, though only after long hesitation, to the President's proposition to have the letter delivered to Kohlhaas by the man whom Nagelschmidt had sent, just as though he had not been arrested, and see whether Kohlhaas would answer it. In accordance with this plan the man, who had been thrown into prison, was taken to the Government Office the next morning. The Governor of the Palace gave him back the letter and, promising him freedom and the remission of the punishment which he had incurred, commanded him to deliver the letter to the horse-dealer as though nothing had happened. As was to be expected, the fellow lent himself to this low trick without hesitation. In apparently mysterious fashion he gained admission to Kohlhaas' room under the pretext of having crabs to sell, with which, in reality, the government clerk had supplied him in the market.

Kohlhaas, who read the letter while the children were playing with the crabs, would certainly have seized the imposter by the collar and handed him over to the soldiers standing before his door, had the circumstances been other than they were. But since, in the existing state of men's minds, even this step was likewise capable of an equivocal interpretation, and as he was fully convinced that nothing in the world could rescue him from the affair in which he was entangled, he gazed sadly into the familiar face of the fellow, asked him where he lived, and bade him return in a few hours' time, when he would inform him of his decision in regard to his master. He told Sternbald, who happened to enter the door, to buy some crabs from the man in the room, and when this business was concluded and both men had gone away without recognizing each other, Kohlhaas sat down and wrote a letter to Nagelschmidt to the following effect: "First, that he accepted his proposition concerning the leadership of his band in Altenburg, and that accordingly, in order to free him from the present arrest in which he was held with his five children, Nagelschmidt should send him a wagon with two horses to Neustadt near Dresden. Also that, to facilitate progress, he would need another team of two horses on the road to Wittenberg, which way, though roundabout, was the only one he could take to come to him, for reasons which it would require too much time to explain. He thought that he would be able to win over by bribery the soldiers who were guarding him, but in case force were necessary he would like to know that he could count on the presence of a couple of stout-hearted, capable, and well-armed men in the suburb of Neustadt. To defray the expenses connected with all these preparations, he was sending Nagelschmidt by his follower a roll of twenty gold crowns concerning the expenditure of which he would settle with him after the affair was concluded. For the rest, Nagelschmidt's presence being unnecessary, he would ask him not to come in person to Dresden to assist at his rescue—nay, rather, he gave him the definite order to remain behind in Altenburg in provisional command of the band which could not be left without a leader."

When the man returned toward evening, he delivered this letter to him, rewarded him liberally, and impressed upon him that he must take good care of it.

Kohlhaas' intention was to go to Hamburg with his five children and there to take ship for the Levant, the East Indies, or the most distant land where the blue sky stretched above people other than those he knew. For his heart, bowed down by grief, had renounced the hope of ever seeing the black horses fattened, even apart from the reluctance that he felt in making common cause with Nagelschmidt to that end.

Hardly had the fellow delivered this answer of the horse-dealer's to the Governor of the Palace when the Lord High Chancellor was deposed, the President, Count Kallheim, was appointed Chief Justice of the Tribunal in his stead, and Kohlhaas was arrested by a special order of the Elector, heavily loaded with chains, and thrown into the city tower. He was brought to trial upon the basis of this letter, which was posted at every street-corner of the city. When a councilor held it up before Kohlhaas at the bar of the Tribunal and asked whether he acknowledged the handwriting, he answered, "Yes;" but to the question as to whether he had anything to say in his defense, he looked down at the ground and replied, "No." He was therefore condemned to be tortured with red-hot pincers by knacker's men, to be drawn and quartered, and his body to be burned between the wheel and the gallows.

Thus stood matters with poor Kohlhaas in Dresden when the Elector of Brandenburg appeared to rescue him from the clutches of arbitrary, superior power, and, in a note laid before the Chancery of State in Dresden, claimed him as a subject of Brandenburg. For the honest City Governor, Sir Heinrich von Geusau, during a walk on the banks of the Spree, had acquainted the Elector with the story of this strange and irreprehensible man, on which occasion, pressed by the questions of the astonished sovereign, he could not avoid mentioning the blame which lay heavy upon the latter's own person through the unwarranted actions of his Arch-Chancellor, Count Siegfried von Kallheim. The Elector was extremely indignant about the matter and after he had called the Arch-Chancellor to account and found that the relationship which he bore to the house of the Tronkas was to blame for it all, he deposed Count Kallheim at once, with more than one token of his displeasure, and appointed Sir Heinrich von Geusau to be Arch-Chancellor in his stead.

Now it so happened that, just at that time, the King of Poland, being at odds with the House of Saxony, for what occasion we do not know, approached the Elector of Brandenburg with repeated and urgent arguments to induce him to make common cause with them against the House of Saxony, and, in consequence of this, the Arch-Chancellor, Sir Geusau, who was not unskilful in such matters, might very well hope that, without imperiling the peace of the whole state to a greater extent than consideration for an individual warrants, he would now be able to fulfil his sovereign's desire to secure justice for Kohlhaas at any cost whatever.

Therefore the Arch-Chancellor did not content himself with demanding, on the score of wholly arbitrary procedure, displeasing to God and man, that Kohlhaas should be unconditionally and immediately surrendered, so that, if guilty of a crime, he might be tried according to the laws of Brandenburg on charges which the Dresden Court might bring against him through an attorney at Berlin; but Sir Heinrich von Geusau even went so far as himself to demand passports for an attorney whom the Elector of Brandenburg wished to send to Dresden in order to secure justice for Kohlhaas against Squire Wenzel Tronka on account of the black horses which had been taken from him on Saxon territory and other flagrant instances of ill-usage and acts of violence. The Chamberlain, Sir Kunz, in the shifting of public offices in Saxony, had been appointed President of the State Chancery, and, hard pressed as he was, desired, for a variety of reasons, not to offend the Court of Berlin. He therefore answered in the name of his sovereign, who had been very greatly cast down by the note he had received, that they wondered at the unfriendliness and unreasonableness which had prompted the government of Brandenburg to contest the right of the Dresden Court to judge Kohlhaas according to their laws for the crimes which he had committed in the land, as it was known to all the world that the latter owned a considerable piece of property in the capital, and he did not himself dispute his qualification as a Saxon citizen.

But as the King of Poland was already assembling an army of five thousand men on the frontier of Saxony to fight for his claims, and as the Arch-Chancellor, Sir Heinrich von Geusau, declared that Kohlhaasenbrück, the place after which the horse-dealer was named, was situated in Brandenburg, and that they would consider the execution of the sentence of death which had been pronounced upon him to be a violation of international law, the Elector of Saxony, upon the advice of the Chamberlain, Sir Kunz himself, who wished to back out of the affair, summoned Prince Christiern of Meissen from his estate, and decided, after a few words with this sagacious nobleman, to surrender Kohlhaas to the Court of Berlin in accordance with their demand.

The Prince, who, although very much displeased with the unseemly blunders which had been committed, was forced to take over the conduct of the Kohlhaas affair at the wish of his hard-pressed master, asked the Elector what charge he now wished to have lodged against the horse-dealer in the Supreme Court at Berlin. As they could not refer to Kohlhaas' fatal letter to Nagelschmidt because of the questionable and obscure circumstances under which it had been written, nor mention the former plundering and burning because of the edict in which the same had been pardoned, the Elector determined to lay before the Emperor's Majesty at Vienna a report concerning the armed invasion of Saxony by Kohlhaas, to make complaint concerning the violation of the public peace established by the Emperor, and to solicit His Majesty, since he was of course not bound by any amnesty, to call Kohlhaas to account therefor before the Court Tribunal at Berlin through an attorney of the Empire.

A week later the horse-dealer, still in chains, was packed into a wagon by the Knight Friedrich of Malzahn, whom the Elector of Brandenburg had sent to Dresden at the head of six troopers; and, together with his five children, who at his request had been collected from various foundling hospitals and orphan asylums, was transported to Berlin.

It so happened that the Elector of Saxony, accompanied by the Chamberlain, Sir Kunz, and his wife, Lady Heloise, daughter of the High Bailiff and sister of the President, not to mention other brilliant ladies and gentlemen, hunting-pages and courtiers, had gone to Dahme at the invitation of the High Bailiff, Count Aloysius of Kallheim, who at that time possessed a large estate on the border of Saxony, and, to entertain the Elector, had organized a large stag-hunt there. Under the shelter of tents gaily decorated with pennons, erected on a hill over against the highroad, the whole company, still covered with the dust of the hunt, was sitting at table, served by pages, while lively music sounded from the trunk of an oak-tree, when Kohlhaas with his escort of troopers came riding slowly along the road from Dresden. The sudden illness of one of Kohlhaas' delicate young children had obliged the Knight of Malzahn, who was his escort, to delay three whole days in Herzberg. Having to answer for this act only to the Prince whom he served, the Knight had not thought it necessary to inform the government of Saxony of the delay. The Elector, with throat half bare, his plumed hat decorated with sprigs of fir, as is the way of hunters, was seated beside Lady Heloise, who had been the first love of his early youth. The charm of the fête which surrounded him having put him in good humor, he said, "Let us go and offer this goblet of wine to the unfortunate man, whoever he may be."

Lady Heloise, casting an entrancing glance at him, got up at once, and, plundering the whole table, filled a silver dish which a page handed her with fruit, cakes, and bread. The entire company had already left the tent in a body, carrying refreshments of every kind, when the High Bailiff came toward them and with an embarrassed air begged them to remain where they were. In answer to the Elector's disconcerted question as to what had happened that he should show such confusion, the High Bailiff turned toward the Chamberlain and answered, stammering, that it was Kohlhaas who was in the wagon. At this piece of news, which none of the company could understand, as it was well known that the horse-dealer had set out six days before, the Chamberlain, Sir Kunz, turning back toward the tent, poured out his glass of wine on the ground. The Elector, flushing scarlet, set his glass down on a plate which a page, at a sign from the Chamberlain, held out to him for this purpose, and while the Knight, Friedrich von Malzahn, respectfully saluting the company, who were unknown to him, passed slowly under the tent ropes that were stretched across the highroad and continued on his way to Dahme, the lords and ladies, at the invitation of the High Bailiff, returned to the tent without taking any further notice of the party. As soon as the Elector had sat down again, the High Bailiff dispatched a messenger secretly to Dahme intending to have the magistrate of that place see to it that the horse-dealer continued his journey immediately; but since the Knight of Malzahn declared positively that, as the day was too far gone, he intended to spend the night in the place, they had to be content to lodge Kohlhaas quietly at a farm-house belonging to the magistrate, which lay off the main road, hidden away among the bushes.

Now it came about toward evening, when all recollection of the incident had been driven from the minds of the lords and ladies by the wine and the abundant dessert they had enjoyed, that the High Bailiff proposed they should again lie in wait for a herd of stags which had shown itself in the vicinity. The whole company took up the suggestion joyfully, and after they had provided themselves with guns went off in pairs, over ditches and hedges, into the near-by forest. Thus it was that the Elector and Lady Heloise, who was hanging on his arm in order to watch the sport, were, to their great astonishment, led by a messenger who had been placed at their service, directly across the court of the house in which Kohlhaas and the Brandenburg troopers were lodged. When Lady Heloise was informed of this she cried, "Your Highness, come!" and playfully concealing inside his silken vest the chain which hung around his neck she added, "Before the crowd follows us let us slip into the farm-house and have a look at the singular man who is spending the night here." The Elector blushed and seized her hand exclaiming, "Heloise! What are you thinking of?" But as she, looking at him with amazement, pulled him along and assured him that no one would ever recognize him in the hunting-costume he had on, and as, moreover, at this very moment a couple of hunting-pages who had already satisfied their curiosity came out of the house, and announced that in truth, on account of an arrangement made by the High Bailiff, neither the Knight nor the horse-dealer knew what company was assembled in the neighborhood of Dahme, the Elector pulled his hat down over his eyes with a smile and said, "Folly, thou rulest the world, and thy throne is a beautiful woman's mouth!"

Kohlhaas was sitting just then on a bundle of straw with his back against the wall, feeding bread and milk to his child who had been taken ill at Herzberg, when Lady Heloise and the Elector entered the farm-house to visit him. To start the conversation, Lady Heloise asked him who he was and what was the matter with the child; also what crime he had committed and where they were taking him with such an escort. Kohlhaas doffed his leather cap to her and, continuing his occupation, made laconic but satisfactory answers to all these questions. The Elector, who was standing behind the hunting-pages, remarked a little leaden locket hanging on a silk string around the horse-dealer's neck, and, since no better topic of conversation offered itself, he asked him what it signified and what was in it. Kohlhaas answered, "Oh, yes, worshipful Sir, this locket!" and with that he slipped it from his neck, opened it, and took out a little piece of paper with writing on it, sealed with a wafer. "There is a strange tale connected with this locket. It may be some seven months ago, on the very day after my wife's funeral—and, as you perhaps know, I had left Kohlhaasenbrück in order to get possession of Squire Tronka, who had done me great wrong—that in the market-town of Jüterbock, through which my expedition led me, the Elector of Saxony and the Elector of Brandenburg had met to discuss I know not what matter. As they had settled it to their liking shortly before evening, they were walking in friendly conversation through the streets of the town in order to take a look at the annual fair which was just being held there with much merrymaking. They came upon a gipsy who was sitting on a stool, telling from the calendar the fortunes of the crowd that surrounded her. The two sovereigns asked her jokingly if she did not have something pleasing to reveal to them too! I had just dismounted with my troop at an inn, and happened to be present in the square where this incident occurred, but as I was standing at the entrance of a church, behind all the people, I could not hear what the strange woman said to the two lords. The people began to whisper to one another laughingly that she did not impart her knowledge to every one, and to crowd together to see the spectacle which was preparing, so that I, really more to make room for the curious than out of curiosity on my part, climbed on a bench behind me which was carved in the entrance of the church. From this point of vantage I could see with perfect ease the two sovereigns and the old woman, who was sitting on the stool before them apparently scribbling something down. But hardly had I caught sight of them, when suddenly she got up, leaning on her crutches, and, gazing around at the people, fixed her eye on me, who had never exchanged a word with her nor ever in all my life consulted her art. Pushing her way over to me through the dense crowd, she said, 'There! If the gentleman wishes to know his fortune, he may ask you about it!' And with these words, your Worship, she stretched out her thin bony hands to me and gave me this paper. All the people turned around in my direction, as I said, amazed, 'Grandam, what in the world is this you are giving me?' After mumbling a lot of inaudible nonsense, amid which, however, to my great surprise, I made out my own name, she answered, 'An amulet, Kohlhaas the horse-dealer; take good car of it; some day it will save your life!'—and vanished. Well," Kohlhaas continued good-naturedly, "to tell the truth, close as was the call in Dresden, I did not lose my life; but how I shall fare in Berlin and whether the charm will help me out there too, the future must show."

At these words the Elector seated himself on a bench, and although to Lady Heloise's frightened question as to what was the matter with him, he answered, "Nothing, nothing at all!"—yet, before she could spring forward and catch him in her arms, he had sunk down unconscious to the floor.

The Knight of Malzahn who entered the room at this moment on some errand, exclaimed, "Good heavens, what is the matter with the gentleman!" Lady Heloise cried, "Bring some water!" The hunting-pages raised the Elector and carried him to a bed in the next room, and the consternation reached its height when the Chamberlain, who had been summoned by a page, declared, after repeated vain efforts to restore him to consciousness, that he showed every sign of having been struck by apoplexy. The Cupbearer sent a mounted messenger to Luckau for the doctor, and then, as the Elector opened his eyes, the High Bailiff had him placed in a carriage and transported at a walk to his hunting-castle near-by; this journey, however, caused two more fainting spells after he had arrived there. Not until late the next morning, on the arrival of the doctor from Luckau, did he recover somewhat, though showing definite symptoms of an approaching nervous fever. As soon as he had returned to consciousness he raised himself on his elbow, and his very first question was, "Where is Kohlhaas?" The Chamberlain, misunderstanding the question, said, as he took his hand, that he might set his heart at rest on the subject of that horrible man, as the latter, after that strange and incomprehensible incident, had by his order remained behind in the farm-house at Dahme with the escort from Brandenburg. Assuring the Elector of his most lively sympathy, and protesting that he had most bitterly reproached his wife for her inexcusable indiscretion in bringing about a meeting between him and this man, the Chamberlain went on to ask what could have occurred during the interview to affect his master so strangely and profoundly.

The Elector answered that he was obliged to confess to him that the sight of an insignificant piece of paper, which the man carried about with him in a leaden locket, was to blame for the whole unpleasant incident which had befallen him. To explain the circumstance, he added a variety of other things which the Chamberlain could not understand, then suddenly, clasping the latter's hand in his own, he assured him that the possession of this paper was of the utmost importance to himself and begged Sir Kunz to mount immediately, ride to Dahme, and purchase the paper for him from the horse-dealer at any price. The Chamberlain, who had difficulty in concealing his embarrassment, assured him that, if this piece of paper had any value for him, nothing in the world was more necessary than to conceal the fact from Kohlhaas, for if the latter should receive an indiscreet intimation of it, all the riches the Elector possessed would not be sufficient to buy it from the hands of this vindictive fellow, whose passion for revenge was insatiable. To calm his master he added that they must try to find another method, and that, as the miscreant probably was not especially attached to it for its own sake, perhaps, by using stratagem, they might get possession of the paper, which was of so much importance to the Elector, through the instrumentality of a third wholly disinterested person.

The Elector, wiping away the perspiration, asked if they could not send immediately to Dahme for this purpose and put a stop to the horse-dealer's being transported further for the present until, by some means or other, they had obtained possession of the paper. The Chamberlain, who could hardly believe his senses, replied that unhappily, according to all probable calculations, the horse-dealer must already have left Dahme and be across the border on the soil of Brandenburg; any attempt to interfere there with his being carried away, or actually to put a stop to it altogether, would give rise to difficulties of the most unpleasant and intricate kind, or even to such as it might perchance be impossible to overcome at all. As the Elector silently sank back on the pillow with a look of utter despair, the Chamberlain asked him what the paper contained and by what surprising and inexplicable chance he knew that the contents concerned himself. At this, however, the Elector cast several ambiguous glances at the Chamberlain, whose obligingness he distrusted on this occasion, and gave no answer. He lay there rigid, with his heart beating tumultuously, and looked down at the corner of the handkerchief which he was holding in his hands as if lost in thought. Suddenly he begged the Chamberlain to call to his room the hunting-page, Stein, an active, clever young gentleman whom he had often employed before in affairs of a secret nature, under the pretense that he had some other business to negotiate with him.

After he had explained the matter to the hunting-page and impressed upon him the importance of the paper which was in Kohlhaas' possession, the Elector asked him whether he wished to win an eternal right to his friendship by procuring this paper for him before the horse-dealer reached Berlin. As soon as the page had to some extent grasped the situation, unusual though it was, he assured his master that he would serve him to the utmost of his ability. The Elector therefore charged him to ride after Kohlhaas, and as it would probably be impossible to approach him with money, Stein should, in a cleverly conducted conversation, proffer him life and freedom in exchange for the paper indeed, if Kohlhaas insisted upon it, he should, though with all possible caution, give him direct assistance in escaping from the hands of the Brandenburg troopers who were convoying him, by furnishing him with horses, men, and money.

The hunting-page, after procuring as a credential a paper written by the Elector's own hand, did immediately set out with several men, and by not sparing the horses' wind he had the good luck to overtake Kohlhaas in a village on the border, where with his five children and the Knight of Malzahn he was eating dinner in the open air before the door of a house. The hunting-page introduced himself to the Knight of Malzahn as a stranger who was passing by and wished to have a look at the extraordinary man whom he was escorting. The Knight at once made him acquainted with Kohlhaas and politely urged him to sit down at the table, and since Malzahn, busied with the preparations for their departure, was obliged to keep coming and going continually, and the troopers were eating their dinner at a table on the other side of the house, the hunting-page soon found an opportunity to reveal to the horse-dealer who he was and on what a peculiar mission he had come to him.

The horse-dealer already knew the name and rank of the man who, at sight of the locket in question, had swooned in the farmhouse at Dahme; and to put the finishing touch to the tumult of excitement into which this discovery had thrown him, he needed only an insight into the secrets contained in the paper which, for many reasons, he was determined not to open out of mere curiosity. He answered that, in consideration of the ungenerous and unprincely treatment he had been forced to endure in Dresden in return for his complete willingness to make every possible sacrifice, he would keep the paper. To the hunting-page's question as to what induced him to make such an extraordinary refusal when he was offered in exchange nothing less than life and liberty, Kohlhaas answered, "Noble Sir, if your sovereign should come to me and say, 'Myself and the whole company of those who help me wield my sceptre I will destroy—destroy, you understand, which is, I admit, the dearest wish that my soul cherishes,' I should nevertheless still refuse to give him the paper which is worth more to him than life, and should say to him, 'You have the authority to send me to the scaffold, but I can cause you pain, and I intend to do so!'" And with these words Kohlhaas, with death staring him in the face, called a trooper to him and told him to take a nice bit of food which had been left in the dish. All the rest of the hour which he spent in the place he acted as though he did not see the young nobleman who was sitting at the table, and not until he climbed up on the wagon did he turn around to the hunting-page again and salute him with a parting glance.

When the Elector received this news his condition grew so much worse that for three fateful days the doctor had grave fears for his life, which was being attacked on so many sides at once. However, thanks to his naturally good constitution, after several weeks spent in pain on the sickbed, he recovered sufficiently, at least, to permit his being placed in a carriage well supplied with pillows and coverings, and brought back to Dresden to take up the affairs of government once more.

As soon as he had arrived in the city he summoned Prince Christiern of Meissen and asked him what had been done about dispatching Judge Eibenmaier, whom the government had thought of sending to Vienna as its attorney in the Kohlhaas affair, in order to lay a complaint before his Imperial Majesty concerning the violation of the public peace proclaimed by the Emperor.

The Prince answered that the Judge, in conformity with the order the Elector had left behind on his departure for Dahme, had set out for Vienna immediately after the arrival of the jurist, Zäuner, whom the Elector of Brandenburg had sent to Dresden as his attorney in order to institute legal proceedings against Squire Wenzel Tronka in regard to the black horses.

The Elector flushed and walked over to his desk, expressing surprise at this haste, since, to his certain knowledge, he had made it clear that because of the necessity for a preliminary consultation with Dr. Luther, who had procured the amnesty for Kohlhaas, he wished to postpone the final departure of Eibenmaier until he should give a more explicit and definite order. At the same time, with an expression of restrained anger, he tossed about some letters and deeds which were lying on his desk. The Prince, after a pause during which he stared in surprise at his master, answered that he was sorry if he had failed to give him satisfaction in this matter; however, he could show the decision of the Council of State enjoining him to send off the attorney at the time mentioned. He added that in the Council of State nothing at all had been said of a consultation with Dr. Luther; that earlier in the affair, it would perhaps have been expedient to pay some regard to this reverend gentleman because of his intervention in Kohlhaas' behalf; but that this was no longer the case, now that the promised amnesty had been violated before the eyes of the world and Kohlhaas had been arrested and surrendered to the Brandenburg courts to be sentenced and executed.

The Elector replied that the error committed in dispatching Eibenmaier was, in fact, not a very serious one; he expressed a wish, however, that, for the present, the latter should not act in Vienna in his official capacity as plaintiff for Saxony, but should await further orders, and begged the Prince to send off to him immediately by a courier the instructions necessary to this end.

The Prince answered that, unfortunately, this order came just one day too late, as Eibenmaier, according to a report which had just arrived that day, had already acted in his capacity as plaintiff and had proceeded with the presentation of the complaint at the State Chancery in Vienna. In answer to the Elector's dismayed question as to how all this was possible in so short a time, he added that three weeks had passed since the departure of this man and that the instructions he had received had charged him to settle the business with all possible dispatch immediately after his arrival in Vienna. A delay, the Prince added, would have been all the more inadvisable in this case, as the Brandenburg attorney, Zäuner, was proceeding against Squire Wenzel Tronka with the most stubborn persistence and had already petitioned the court for the provisional removal of the black horses from the hands of the knacker with a view to their future restoration to good condition, and, in spite of all the arguments of the opposite side, had carried his point.

The Elector, ringing the bell, said, "No matter; it is of no importance," and turning around again toward the Prince asked indifferently how other things were going in Dresden and what had occurred during his absence. Then, incapable of hiding his inner state of mind, he saluted him with a wave of the hand and dismissed him.

That very same day the Elector sent him a written demand for all the official documents concerning Kohlhaas, under the pretext that, on account of the political importance of the affair, he wished to go over it himself. As he could not bear to think of destroying the man from whom alone he could receive information concerning the secrets contained in the paper, he composed an autograph letter to the Emperor; in this he affectionately and urgently requested that, for weighty reasons, which possibly he would explain to him in greater detail after a little while, he be allowed to withdraw for a time, until a further decision had been reached, the complaint which Eibenmaier had entered against Kohlhaas.

The Emperor, in a note drawn up by the State Chancery, replied that the change which seemed suddenly to have taken place in the Elector's mind astonished him exceedingly; that the report which had been furnished him on the part of Saxony had made the Kohlhaas affair a matter which concerned the entire Holy Roman Empire; that, in consequence, he, the Emperor, as head of the same, had felt it his duty to appear before the house of Brandenburg in this, as plaintiff in this affair, and that, therefore, since the Emperor's counsel, Franz Müller, had gone to Berlin in the capacity of attorney in order to call Kohlhaas to account for the violation of the public peace, the complaint could in no wise be withdrawn now and the affair must take its course in conformity with the law.

This letter completely crushed the Elector and, to his utter dismay, private communications from Berlin reached him a short time after, announcing the institution of the lawsuit before the Supreme Court at Berlin and containing the remark that Kohlhaas, in spite of all the efforts of the lawyer assigned him, would in all probability end on the scaffold. The unhappy sovereign determined, therefore, to make one more effort, and in an autograph letter begged the Elector of Brandenburg to spare Kohlhaas' life. He alleged as pretext that the amnesty solemnly promised to this man did not lawfully permit the execution of a death sentence upon him; he assured the Elector that, in spite of the apparent severity with which Kohlhaas had been treated in Saxony, it had never been his intention to allow the latter to die, and described how wretched he should be if the protection which they had pretended to be willing to afford the man from Berlin should, by an unexpected turn of affairs, prove in the end to be more detrimental to him than if he had remained in Dresden and his affair had been decided according to the laws of Saxony.

The Elector of Brandenburg, to whom much of this declaration seemed ambiguous and obscure, answered that the energy with which the attorney of his Majesty the Emperor was proceeding made it absolutely out of the question for him to conform to the wish expressed by the Elector of Saxony and depart from the strict precepts of the law. He remarked that the solicitude thus displayed really went too far, inasmuch as the complaint against Kohlhaas on account of the crimes which had been pardoned in the amnesty had, as a matter of fact, not been entered at the Supreme Court at Berlin by him, the sovereign who had granted the amnesty, but by the supreme head of the Empire who was in no wise bound thereby. At the same time he represented to him how necessary it was to make a fearful example of Kohlhaas in view of the continued outrages of Nagelschmidt, who with unheard-of boldness was already extending his depredations as far as Brandenburg, and begged him, in case he refused to be influenced by these considerations, to apply to His Majesty the Emperor himself, since, if a decree was to be issued in favor of Kohlhaas, this could only be rendered after a declaration on his Majesty's part.

The Elector fell ill again with grief and vexation over all these unsuccessful attempts, and one morning, when the Chamberlain came to pay him a visit, he showed him the letters which he had written to the courts of Vienna and Berlin in the effort to prolong Kohlhaas' life and thus at least gain time in which to get possession of the paper in the latter's hands. The Chamberlain threw himself on his knees before him and begged him by all that he held sacred and dear to tell him what this paper contained. The Elector bade him bolt the doors of the room and sit down on the bed beside him, and after he had grasped his hand and, with a sigh, pressed it to his heart, he began as follows: "Your wife, as I hear, has already told you that the Elector of Brandenburg and I, on the third day of the conference that we held at Jüterbock, came upon a gipsy, and the Elector, lively as he is by nature, determined to destroy by a jest in the presence of all the people the fame of this fantastic woman, whose art had, inappropriately enough, just been the topic of conversation at dinner. He walked up to her table with his arms crossed and demanded from her a sign—one that could be put to the test that very day—to prove the truth of the fortune she was about to tell him, pretending that, even if she were the Roman Sibyl herself, he could not believe her words without it. The woman, hastily taking our measure from head to foot, said that the sign would be that, even before we should leave, the big horned roebuck which the gardener's son was raising in the park, would come to meet us in the market-place where we were standing at that moment. Now you must know that this roebuck, which was destined for the Dresden kitchen, was kept behind lock and key in an inclosure fenced in with high boards and shaded by the oak-trees of the park; and since, moreover, on account of other smaller game and birds, the park in general and also the garden leading to it, were kept carefully locked, it was absolutely impossible to understand how the animal could carry out this strange prediction and come to meet us in the square where we were standing. Nevertheless the Elector, afraid that some trick might be behind it and determined for the sake of the joke to give the lie once and for all to everything else that she might say, sent to the castle, after a short consultation with me, and ordered that the roebuck be instantly killed and prepared for the table within the next few days. Then he turned back to the woman before whom this matter had been transacted aloud, and said, 'Well, go ahead! What have you to disclose to me of the future?' The woman, looking at his hand, said, 'Hail, my Elector and Sovereign! Your Grace will reign for a long time, the house from which you spring will long endure, and your descendants will be great and glorious and will come to exceed in power all the other princes and sovereigns of the world.'

"The Elector, after a pause in which he looked thoughtfully at the woman, said in an undertone, as he took a step toward me, that he was almost sorry now that he had sent off a messenger to ruin the prophecy; and while amid loud rejoicing the money rained down in heaps into the woman's lap from the hands of the knights who followed the Elector, the latter, after feeling in his pocket and adding a gold piece on his own account, asked if the salutation which she was about to reveal to me also had such a silvery sound as his. The woman opened a box that stood beside her and in a leisurely, precise way arranged the money in it according to kind and quantity; then she closed it again, shaded her eyes with her hand as if the sun annoyed her, and looked at me. I repeated the question I had asked her and, while she examined my hand, I added jokingly to the Elector, 'To me, so it seems, she has nothing really agreeable to announce!' At that she seized her crutches, raised herself slowly with their aid from her stool, and, pressing close to me with her hands held before her mysteriously, she whispered audibly in my ear, 'No!'—'Is that so?' I asked confused, and drew back a step before the figure, who with a look cold and lifeless as though from eyes of marble, seated herself once more on the stool behind her;—'from what quarter does danger menace my house?' The woman, taking a piece of charcoal and a paper in her hand and crossing her knees, asked whether she should write it down for me; and as I, really embarrassed, though only because under the existing circumstances there was nothing else for me to do, answered, 'Yes, do so,' she replied, 'Very well! Three things I will write down for you—the name of the last ruler of your house, the year in which he will lose his throne, and the name of the man who through the power of arms will seize it for himself.' Having done this before the eyes of all the people she arose, sealed the paper with a wafer, which she moistened in her withered mouth, and pressed upon it a leaden seal ring which she wore on her middle finger. And as I, curious beyond all words, as you can well imagine, was about to seize the paper, she said, 'Not so, Your Highness!' and turned and raised one of her crutches; 'from that man there, the one with the plumed hat, standing on the bench at the entrance of the church behind all the people—from him you shall redeem it, if it so please you!' And with these words, before I had clearly grasped what she was saying, she left me standing in the square, speechless with astonishment, and, clapping shut the box that stood behind her and slinging it over her back, she disappeared in the crowd of people surrounding us, so that I could no longer watch what she was doing. But at this moment, to my great consolation, I must admit, there appeared the knight whom the Elector had sent to the castle, and reported, with a smile hovering on his lips, that the roebuck had been killed and dragged off to the kitchen by two hunters before his very eyes. The Elector, gaily placing his arm in mine with the intention of leading me away from the square, said, 'Well then, the prophecy was a commonplace swindle and not worth the time and money which it has cost us!' But how great was our astonishment when, even before he had finished speaking, a cry went up around the whole square, and the eyes of all turned toward a large butcher's dog trotting along from the castle yard. In the kitchen he had seized the roebuck by the neck as a fair prize, and, pursued by men-servants and maids, dropped the animal on the ground three paces in front of us. Thus indeed the woman's prophecy, which was the pledge for the truth of all that she had uttered, was fulfilled, and the roebuck, although dead to be sure, had come to the market-place to meet us. The lightning which falls from heaven on a winter's day cannot annihilate more completely than this sight did me, and my first endeavor, as soon as I had excused myself from the company which surrounded me, was to discover immediately the whereabouts of the man with the plumed hat whom the woman had pointed out to me; but none of my people, though sent out on a three days' continuous search, could give me even the remotest kind of information concerning him. And then, friend Kunz, a few weeks ago in the farm-house at Dahme, I saw the man with my own eyes!"

With these words he let go of the Chamberlain's hand and, wiping away the perspiration, sank back again on the couch. The Chamberlain, who considered it a waste of effort to attempt to contradict the Elector's opinion of the incident or to try to make him adopt his own view of the matter, begged him by all means to try to get possession of the paper and afterward to leave the fellow to his fate. But the Elector answered that he saw absolutely no way of doing so, although the thought of having to do without it or perhaps even seeing all knowledge of it perish with this man, brought him to the verge of misery and despair. When asked by his friend whether he had made any attempts to discover the person of the gipsy-woman herself, the Elector replied that the Government Office, in consequence of an order which he had issued under a false pretext, had been searching in vain for this woman throughout the Electorate; in view of these facts, for reasons, however, which he refused to explain in detail, he doubted whether she could ever be discovered in Saxony.

Now it happened that the Chamberlain wished to go to Berlin on account of several considerable pieces of property in the Neumark of Brandenburg which his wife had fallen heir to from the estate of the Arch-Chancellor, Count Kallheim, who had died shortly after being deposed. As Sir Kunz really loved the Elector, he asked, after reflecting for a short time, whether the latter would leave the matter to his discretion; and when his master, pressing his hand affectionately to his breast, answered, "Imagine that you are myself, and secure the paper for me!" the Chamberlain turned over his affairs to a subordinate, hastened his departure by several days, left his wife behind, and set out for Berlin, accompanied only by a few servants.

Kohlhaas, as we have said, had meanwhile arrived in Berlin, and by special order of the Elector of Brandenburg had been placed in a prison for nobles, where, together with his five children, he was made as comfortable as circumstances permitted. Immediately after the appearance of the Imperial attorney from Vienna the horse-dealer was called to account before the bar of the Supreme Court for the violation of the public peace proclaimed throughout the Empire, and although in his answer he objected that, by virtue of the agreement concluded with the Elector of Saxony at Lützen, he could not be prosecuted for the armed invasion of that country and the acts of violence committed at that time, he was nevertheless told for his information that His Majesty the Emperor, whose attorney was making the complaint in this case, could not take that into account. And indeed, after the situation had been explained to him and he had been told that, to offset this, complete satisfaction would be rendered to him in Dresden in his suit against Squire Wenzel Tronka, he very soon acquiesced in the matter.

Thus it happened that, precisely on the day of the arrival of the Chamberlain, judgment was pronounced, and Kohlhaas was condemned to lose his life by the sword, which sentence, however, in the complicated state of affairs, no one believed would be carried out, in spite of its mercy. Indeed the whole city, knowing the good will which the Elector bore Kohlhaas, confidently hoped to see it commuted by an electoral decree to a mere, though possibly long and severe, term of imprisonment.

The Chamberlain, who nevertheless realized that no time was to be lost if the commission given him by his master was to be accomplished, set about his business by giving Kohlhaas an opportunity to get a good look at him, dressed as he was in his ordinary court costume, one morning when the horse-dealer was standing at the window of his prison innocently gazing at the passers-by. As he concluded from a sudden movement of his head that he had noticed him, and with great pleasure observed particularly that he put his hand involuntarily to that part of the chest where the locket was lying, he considered that what had taken place at that moment in Kohlhaas' soul was a sufficient preparation to allow him to go a step further in the attempt to gain possession of the paper. He therefore sent for an old woman who hobbled around on crutches, selling old clothes; he had noticed her in the streets of Berlin among a crowd of other rag-pickers, and in age and costume she seemed to him to correspond fairly well to the woman described to him by the Elector of Saxony. On the supposition that Kohlhaas probably had not fixed very deeply in mind the features of the old gipsy, of whom he had had but a fleeting vision as she handed him the paper, he determined to substitute the aforesaid woman for her and, if it were practicable, to have her act the part of the gipsy before Kohlhaas. In accordance with this plan and in order to fit her for the role, he informed her in detail of all that had taken place in Jüterbock between the Elector and the gipsy, and, as he did not know how far the latter had gone in her declarations to Kohlhaas, he did not forget to impress particularly upon the woman the three mysterious items contained in the paper. After he had explained to her what she must disclose in disconnected and incoherent fashion, about certain measures which had been taken to get possession, either by strategy or by force, of this paper which was of the utmost importance to the Saxon court, he charged her to demand of Kohlhaas that he should give the paper to her to keep during a few fateful days, on the pretext that it was no longer safe with him.

As was to be expected, the woman undertook the execution of this business at once on the promise of a considerable reward, a part of which the Chamberlain, at her demand, had to pay over to her in advance. As the mother of Herse, the groom who had fallen at Mühlberg, had permission from the government to visit Kohlhaas at times, and this woman had already known her for several months, she succeeded a few days later in gaining access to the horse-dealer by means of a small gratuity to the warden.

But when the woman entered his room, Kohlhaas, from a seal ring that she wore on her hand and a coral chain that hung round her neck, thought that he recognized in her the very same old gipsy-woman who had handed him the paper in Jüterbock; and since probability is not always on the side of truth, it so happened that here something had occurred which we will indeed relate, but at the same time, to those who wish to question it we must accord full liberty to do so. The Chamberlain had made the most colossal blunder, and in the aged old-clothes woman, whom he had picked up in the streets of Berlin to impersonate the gipsy, he had hit upon the very same mysterious gipsy-woman whom he wished to have impersonated. At least, while leaning on her crutches and stroking the cheeks of the children who, intimidated by her singular appearance, were pressing close to their father, the woman informed the latter that she had returned to Brandenburg from Saxony some time before, and that after an unguarded question which the Chamberlain had hazarded in the streets of Berlin about the gipsy-woman who had been in Jüterbock in the spring of the previous year, she had immediately pressed forward to him, and under a false name had offered herself for the business which he wished to see done.

The horse-dealer remarked such a strange likeness between her and his dead wife Lisbeth that he might have asked the old woman whether she were his wife's grandmother; for not only did her features and her hands with fingers still shapely and beautiful—and especially the use she made of them when speaking—remind him vividly of Lisbeth; he even noticed on her neck a mole like one with which his wife's neck was marked. With his thoughts in a strange whirl he urged the gipsy to sit down on a chair and asked what it could possibly be that brought her to him on business for the Chamberlain.

While Kohlhaas' old dog snuffed around her knees and wagged his tail as she gently patted his head, the woman answered that she had been commissioned by the Chamberlain to inform him what the three questions of importance for the Court of Saxony were, to which the paper contained the mysterious answer; to warn him of a messenger who was then in Berlin for the purpose of gaining possession of it; and to demand the paper from him on the pretext that it was no longer safe next his heart where he was carrying it. She said that the real purpose for which she had come, however, was to tell him that the threat to get the paper away from him by strategy or by force was an absurd and empty fraud; that under the protection of the Elector of Brandenburg, in whose custody he was, he need not have the least fear for its safety; that the paper was indeed much safer with him than with her, and that he should take good care not to lose possession of it by giving it up to any one, no matter on what pretext. Nevertheless, she concluded, she considered it would be wise to use the paper for the purpose for which she had given it to him at the fair in Jüterbock, to lend a favorable ear to the offer which had been made to him on the frontier through Squire Stein, and in return for life and liberty to surrender the paper, which could be of no further use to him, to the Elector of Saxony.

Kohlhaas, who was exulting over the power which was thus afforded him to wound the heel of his enemy mortally at the very moment when it was treading him in the dust, made answer, "Not for the world, grandam, not for the world!" He pressed the old woman's hand warmly and only asked to know what sort of answers to the tremendous questions were contained in the paper. Taking on her lap the youngest child, who had crouched at her feet, the woman said, "Not for the world, Kohlhaas the horse-dealer, but for this pretty, fair-haired little lad!" and with that she laughed softly at the child, petted and kissed him while he stared at her in wide-eyed surprise, and with her withered hands gave him an apple which she had in her pocket. Kohlhaas answered, in some confusion, that the children themselves, when they were grown, would approve his conduct, and that he could do nothing of greater benefit to them and their grandchildren than to keep the paper. He asked, furthermore, who would insure him against a new deception after the experience he had been through, and whether, in the end, he would not be making a vain sacrifice of the paper to the Elector, as had lately happened in the case of the band of troops which he had collected in Lützen. "If I've once caught a man breaking his word," said he, "I never exchange another with him; and nothing but your command, positive and unequivocal, shall separate me, good grandam, from this paper through which I have been granted satisfaction in such a wonderful fashion for all I have suffered."

The woman set the child down on the floor again and said that in many respects he was right, and that he could do or leave undone what he wished; and with that she took up her crutches again and started to go. Kohlhaas repeated his question regarding the contents of the wonderful paper; she answered hastily that, of course, he could open it, although it would be pure curiosity on his part. He wished to find out about a thousand other things yet, before she left him—who she really was, how she came by the knowledge resident within her, why she had refused to give the magic paper to the Elector for whom it had been written after all, and among so many thousand people had handed it precisely to him, Kohlhaas, who had never consulted her art.

Now it happened that, just at that moment, a noise was heard, caused by several police officials who were mounting the stairway, so that the woman, seized with sudden apprehension at being found by them in these quarters, exclaimed, "Good-by for the present, Kohlhaas, good-by for the present. When we meet again you shall not lack information concerning all these things." With that she turned toward the door, crying, "Farewell, children, farewell!" Then she kissed the little folks one after the other, and went off. In the mean time the Elector of Saxony, abandoned to his wretched thoughts, had called in two astrologers, Oldenholm and Olearius by name, who at that time enjoyed a great reputation in Saxony, and had asked their advice concerning the mysterious paper which was of such importance to him and all his descendants. After making a profound investigation of several days' duration in the tower of the Dresden palace, the men could not agree as to whether the prophecy referred to remote centuries or, perhaps, to the present time, with a possible reference to the King of Poland, with whom the relations were still of a very warlike nature. The disquietude, not to say the despair, in which the unhappy sovereign was plunged, was only increased by such learned disputes, and finally was so intensified as to seem to his soul wholly intolerable. In addition, just at this time the Chamberlain charged his wife that before she left for Berlin, whither she was about to follow him, she should adroitly inform the Elector, that, after the failure of an attempt, which he had made with the help of an old woman who had kept out of sight ever since, there was but slight hope of securing the paper in Kohlhaas' possession, inasmuch as the death sentence pronounced against the horse-dealer had now at last been signed by the Elector of Brandenburg after a minute examination of all the legal documents, and the day of execution already set for the Monday after Palm Sunday. At this news the Elector, his heart torn by grief and remorse, shut himself up in his room like a man in utter despair and, tired of life, refused for two days to take food; on the third day he suddenly disappeared from Dresden after sending a short communication to the Government Office with word that he was going to the Prince of Dessau's to hunt.

Where he actually did go and whether he did wend his way toward Dessau, we shall not undertake to say, as the chronicles—

which we have diligently compared before reporting events—at this point contradict and offset one another in a very peculiar manner. So much is certain: the Prince of Dessau was incapable of hunting, as he was at this time lying ill in Brunswick at the residence of his uncle, Duke Henry, and it is also certain that Lady Heloise on the evening of the following day arrived in Berlin at the house of her husband, Sir Kunz, the Chamberlain, in the company of a certain Count von Königstein whom she gave out to be her cousin.

In the mean time, on the order of the Elector of Brandenburg, the death sentence was read to Kohlhaas, his chains were removed, and the papers concerning his property, to which papers his right had been denied in Dresden, were returned to him. When the councilors whom the court had dispatched to him asked what disposition he wished to have made of his property after his death, with the help of a notary he made out a will in favor of his children and appointed his honest friend, the bailiff at Kohlhaasenbrück, to be their guardian. After that, nothing could match the peace and contentment of his last days. For in consequence of a singular decree extraordinary issued by the Elector, the prison in which he was kept was soon after thrown open and free entrance was allowed day and night to all his friends, of whom he possessed a great many in the city. He even had the further satisfaction of seeing the theologian, Jacob Freising, enter his prison as a messenger from Dr. Luther, with a letter from the latter's own hand—without doubt a very remarkable document which, however, has since been lost—and of receiving the blessed Holy Communion at the hands of this reverend gentleman in the presence of two deans of Brandenburg, who assisted him in administering it.

Amid general commotion in the city, which could not even yet be weaned from the hope of seeing him saved by an electoral rescript, there now dawned the fateful Monday after Palm Sunday, on which Kohlhaas was to make atonement to the world for the all-too-rash attempt to procure justice for himself within it. Accompanied by a strong guard and conducted by the theologian, Jacob Freising, he was just leaving the gate of his prison with his two lads in his arms—for this favor he had expressly requested at the bar of the court—when among a sorrowful throng of acquaintances, who were pressing his hands in farewell, there stepped up to him, with haggard face, the castellan of the Elector's palace, and gave him a paper which he said an old woman had put in his hands for him. The latter, looking in surprise at the man, whom he scarcely knew, opened the paper. The seal pressed upon the wafer had reminded him at once of the frequently mentioned gipsy-woman, but who can describe the astonishment which filled him when he found the following information contained in it: "Kohlhaas, the Elector of Saxony is in Berlin; he has already preceded you to the place of execution, and, if you care to know, can be recognized by a hat with blue and white plumes. The purpose for which he comes I do not need to tell you. He intends, as soon as you are buried, to have the locket dug up and the paper in it opened and read. Your Lisbeth."

Kohlhaas turned to the castellan in the utmost astonishment and asked him if he knew the marvelous woman who had given him the note. But just as the castellan started to answer "Kohlhaas, the woman—" and then hesitated strangely in the middle of his sentence, the horse-dealer was borne away by the procession which moved on again at that moment, and could not make out what the man, who seemed to be trembling in every limb, finally uttered.

When Kohlhaas arrived at the place of execution he found there the Elector of Brandenburg and his suite, among whom was the Arch-Chancellor, Sir Heinrich von Geusau, halting on horseback, in the midst of an innumerable crowd of people. On the sovereign's right was the Imperial attorney, Franz Müller, with a copy of the death sentence in his hand; on his left was his own attorney, the jurist Anton Zäuner, with the decree of the Court Tribunal at Dresden. In the middle of the half circle formed by the people stood a herald with a bundle of articles, and the two black horses, fat and glossy, pawing the ground impatiently. For the Arch-Chancellor, Sir Heinrich, had won the suit instituted at Dresden in the name of his master without yielding a single point to Squire Wenzel Tronka. After the horses had been made honorable once more by having a banner waved over their heads, and taken from the knacker, who was feeding them, they had been fattened by the Squire's servants and then, in the market-place in Dresden, had been turned over to the attorney in the presence of a specially appointed commission. Accordingly when Kohlhaas, accompanied by his guard, advanced to the mound where the Elector was awaiting him, the latter said, "Well, Kohlhaas, this is the day on which you receive justice that is your due. Look, I here deliver to you all that was taken from you by force at the Tronka Castle which I, as your sovereign, was bound to procure for you again; here are the black horses, the neck-cloth, the gold gulden, the linen—everything down to the very amount of the bill for medical attention furnished your groom, Herse, who fell at Mühlberg. Are you satisfied with me?"

Kohlhaas set the two children whom he was carrying in his arms down on the ground beside him, and with eyes sparkling with astonished pleasure read the decree which was handed to him at a sign from the Arch-Chancellor. When he also found in it a clause condemning Squire Wenzel Tronka to a punishment of two years' imprisonment, his feelings completely overcame him and he sank down on his knees at some distance from the Elector, with his hands folded across his breast. Rising and laying his hand on the knee of the Arch-Chancellor, he joyfully assured him that his dearest wish on earth had been fulfilled; then he walked over to the horses, examined them and patted their plump necks, and, coming back to the Chancellor, declared with a smile that he was going to present them to his two sons, Henry and Leopold!

The Chancellor, Sir Heinrich von Geusau, looking graciously down upon him from his horse, promised him in the name of the Elector that his last wish should be held sacred and asked him also to dispose of the other articles contained in the bundle, as seemed good to him. Whereupon Kohlhaas called out from the crowd Herse's old mother, whom he had caught sight of in the square, and, giving her the things, said, "Here, grandmother, these belong to you!" The indemnity for the loss of Herse was with the money in the bundle, and this he presented to her also, as a gift to provide care and comfort for her old age. The Elector cried, "Well, Kohlhaas the horse-dealer, now that satisfaction has been rendered you in such fashion, do you, for your part, prepare to give satisfaction to His Majesty the Emperor, whose attorney is standing here, for the violation of the peace he had proclaimed!" Taking off his hat and throwing it on the ground, Kohlhaas said that he was ready to do so. He lifted the children once more from the ground and pressed them to his breast; then he gave them over to the bailiff of Kohlhaasenbrück, and while the latter, weeping quietly, led them away from the square, Kohlhaas advanced to the block.

He was just removing his neck-cloth and baring his chest when, throwing a hasty glance around the circle formed by the crowd, he caught sight of the familiar face of the man with blue and white plumes, who was standing quite near him between two knights whose bodies half hid him from view. With a sudden stride which surprised the guard surrounding him, Kohlhaas walked close up to the man, untying the locket from around his neck as he did so. He took out the paper, unsealed it, and read it through; then, without moving his eyes from the man with blue and white plumes, who was already beginning to indulge in sweet hopes, he stuck the paper in his mouth and swallowed it.

At this sight the man with blue and white plumes was seized with convulsions and sank down unconscious. While his companions bent over him in consternation and raised him from the ground, Kohlhaas turned toward the scaffold, where his head fell under the axe of the executioner.

Here ends the story of Kohlhaas. Amid the general lamentations of the people his body was placed in a coffin, and while the bearers raised it from the ground and bore it away to the graveyard in the suburbs for decent burial, the Elector of Brandenburg called to him the sons of the dead man and dubbed them knights, telling the Arch-Chancellor that he wished them to be educated in his school for pages.

The Elector of Saxony, shattered in body and mind, returned shortly afterward to Dresden; details of his subsequent career there must be sought in history.

Some hale and happy descendants of Kohlhaas, however, were still living in Mecklenburg in the last century.

Books published by Mondial

Rougon-Macquart Series:

Emile Zola: The Fortune of the Rougons
(ISBN 1595690107 / 9781595690104)

Emile Zola: The Fat and the Thin (The Belly of Paris)
(ISBN 1595690522 / 9781595690524)

Emile Zola: Abbe Mouret's Transgression (The Sin of the Abbé Mouret)
(ISBN 1595690506 / 9781595690500)

Emile Zola: The Dream
(ISBN 1595690492 / 9781595690494)

Emile Zola: A Love Episode (A Page of Love)
(ISBN 1595690271 / 9781595690272)

Emile Zola: The Conquest of Plassans
(ISBN 1595690484 / 9781595690487)

Emile Zola: The Joy of Life (Zest for Life)
(ISBN 1595690476 / ISBN 9781595690470)

Emile Zola: Doctor Pascal
(ISBN 1595690514 / 9781595690517)

Emile Zola: His Excellency (His Excellency, Eugene Rougon)
(ISBN 1595690557 / 9781595690555)

Emile Zola: Money
(ISBN 9781595690630)

Other books:

Emile Zola: Fruitfulness
(ISBN 1595690182 / 9781595690180)

Victor Hugo: The Man Who Laughs (By Order of the King)
(ISBN 1595690131 / 9781595690135)

Victor Hugo: History of a Crime
(ISBN 1595690204 / 9781595690203)

Honoré de Balzac: Ursula (Ursule Mirouet)
(ISBN 1595690530 / 9781595690531)

Honoré de Balzac: Maitre Cornelius
(ISBN 1595690174 / 9781595690173)

Anatole France: Penguin Island
(ISBN 1595690298 / 9781595690296)

Anatole France: The Crime of Sylvestre Bonnard (ISBN 9781595690593)

Gustave Flaubert: Salammbo (Salambo)
(ISBN 1595690352 / 9781595690357)

Romain Rolland: Pierre and Luce (ISBN 9781595690609)

Jules Verne: An Antarctic Mystery (The Sphinx of the Ice Fields)
(ISBN 1595690549 / 9781595690548)

Andre Gide: Strait is the Gate (André Gide: La Portre étroite;
ISBN 9781595690623)

André Gide: Prometheus Illbound (ISBN 9781595690807)

André Gide: Recollections of Oscar Wilde (ISBN 9781595690814)

Agatha Christie: Two Novels (The Mysterious Affair at Styles. The Secret Adversary.) (ISBN 1595690417 / 9781595690418)

Johann Wolfgang von Goethe: The Sorrows of Young Werther (ISBN 159569045X / 9781595690456)

Jack London: War of the Classes. Revolution. The Shrinkage of the Planet. (ISBN 1595690409 / 9781595690401)

Jack London: Before Adam. Children of the Frost. (ISBN 1595690395 / 9781595690395)

Jack London: The Iron Heel (ISBN 1595690379 / 9781595690371)

Oscar Wilde, Anonymous: Teleny or The Reverse of the Medal (Gay erotic classic; ISBN 1595690360 / 9781595690364)

Martin Andersen Nexo: Pelle the Conqueror (Complete Edition) (ISBN 159569028X / 9781595690289)

Martin Andersen Nexo: Ditte Everywoman (Complete Edition: Girl Alive. Daughter of Man. Towards the Stars.) (ISBN 9781595690333)

Susan Coolidge: Clover (ISBN 1595690263 / 9781595690265)

Jerome K. Jerome: Idle Thoughts of an Idle Fellow (ISBN 1595690247 / 9781595690241)

Malama Katulwende: Bitterness (An African Novel from Zambia) (ISBN 159569031X / 9781595690319)

Sigmund Freud: Dream Psychology (Psychoanalysis for Beginners) (ISBN 1595690166 / 9781595690166)

Theodor Storm, Adelbert von Chamisso, Adalbert Stifter: Famous German Novellas of the 19th Century (Immensee. Peter Schlemihl. Brigitta) (ISBN 159569014X / 9781595690142)

Getrude Stein: Three Lives (With an Introduction by Carl Van Vechten - ISBN 1595690425 / 9781595690425)

Gabriele D'Annunzio: The Child of Pleasure (ISBN 9781595690581)

Frederick (Friedrich) Engels: Socialism: Utopian and Scientific (Appendix: The Mark; Preface: Karl Marx) (ISBN 1595690468 / 9781595690463)

Karl Marx: The Eighteenth Brumaire of Louis Bonaparte (ISBN 1595690239 / 9781595690234)

Carl Van Vechten: Firecrackers (ISBN 9781595690685)

Bruce Kellner: Winter Ridge (ISBN 9781595690692)

Oscar Wilde: The Critic as Artist. Upon the Importance of Doing Nothing and Discussing Everything. (ISBN 9781595690821)

Heinrich Heine: Germany. A Winter Tale (Deutschland. Ein Wintermärchen) ISBN 9781595690715

Theodor Storm: The Rider of the White Horse (The Dykemaster) ISBN 9781595690746